SAVING THE WHITE COUGAR

HEART OF THE COUGAR, BOOK 10

TERRY SPEAR

WILDE INK PUBLISHING

PUBLISHED BY:

Wilde Ink Publishing

Saving the White Cougar

Copyright © 2021 by Terry Spear

Cover Copyright by Terry Spear

Discover more about Terry Spear at:

http://www.terryspear.com/

Print ISBN: 978-1-63311-071-7

Ebook ISBN: 978-1-63311-069-4

SYNOPSIS

Stella White never believed that going on a cougar run would be such a dangerous excursion, painful, punishing, and pleasurable in the end. She realized that sometimes she just needed to get through the bad stuff to get to the good stuff and that meant meeting Ted Weekum, ranch foreman, and the kind of cowboy she'd only dreamed of.

Ted Weekum was visiting with his brother at the ranch when he thought he saw a white flash of fur, but it wasn't until hunters started shooting up the place, claiming they'd shot a white cougar did the notion sink in that the cougar could be one of their own shifter kind. But a white cougar? Unheard of. And yet when he went to save her life—that's exactly what he found. A rare white cougar. Unclaimed. Unmated. The right age. The stars had aligned right that night.

But the hunters aren't through with hunting down the wounded white cougar, or Stella White.

Thanks to Kari Schatteles who sent me the article about an extremely rare white cougar, a young male with leucism, caught on a trail camera in Brazil. Thanks again, Kari! You were my inspiration for writing Saving the White Cougar!

CHAPTER 1

*S*tella White was one of the extremely rare white cougars in existence. She was leucistic, not albino. Yet she wasn't *just* a white cougar, but a shifter too. And she'd never met one of *her* kind before either.

Most of the time, being a white cougar didn't give her trouble because she ran in her cougar coat when she felt the urge—*after* work hours and mostly at dusk or dawn—where no one lived or worked or played. Until today.

When she went into work on Friday, she had her whole day planned—take care of all the legal duties she needed to accomplish as a paralegal for a high-powered lawyer firm, humans only. Have dinner home alone, since she didn't have a current boyfriend. No other cougars were living in Grand Junction, Colorado, and so she was stuck dating humans from time to time. Just like cougar shifters could be, the humans she'd dated hadn't been faithful either. She enjoyed having a boyfriend and dating. She wasn't that into being single. But she did have the one major drawback. She was a shifter and turning a human into one of her kind wasn't a great idea. Now, if she found one she was totally into, she might change her mind. But she hadn't found anyone like that yet.

After work, she was running as a cougar. With the passing days approaching Halloween, it was getting darker earlier. She would go before sunset to enjoy a rock-climbing expedition and check out some waterfalls she had seen on a map. Rainbow Falls were situated about four miles from the rocks she would climb. During a search for places she could safely run as a cougar, she had checked out the location earlier in the week. A place that had signs posted: No Trespassing, No Hunting allowed. Almost as good as a wildlife reserve. That's what she was looking for.

"Are you going out to dinner with Frankie?" Tori Stone was another paralegal at Brown and Sons and Stella thought she was interested in dating her ex-boyfriend.

"Nope. We're through. You can have him if you want. But I have to warn you, he has a roving eye."

"Nah, I'm not interested," Tori said, but Stella knew differently.

The guy was cute, but Stella wasn't into a guy who couldn't stick with the woman he was currently dating. It was totally rude the way he engaged in conversations with women all the time when he was on a date with Stella as if he were available and looking for a new hookup.

Stella glanced at the clock. *Time to go.* "See you Monday."

"See you."

First, Stella dropped by her apartment to change out of her suit pants and into jeans, hiking boots, and a long-sleeved T-shirt that said: Cougars make the best friends. She threw on her jeans jacket, needing just something light for the trip to the place she planned to run at. She thought about making a quick grilled chicken sandwich, but she wanted to hit the road, do her cougar run, and she could make dinner when she returned home.

She loved exploring new places, hoping she would find the idyllic spot to call her own as a cougar—not for real, but just for visits. It was pumpkin time, but she couldn't wait for the snow to fall. She loved the snow because that's when she could hide the best—white on white, nothing could be better.

Though she really didn't stand out all that much at any time of the year as long as she was in the tall grasses or forests. She would leap into a tree and practically disappear. Maybe not as much as a tan cougar would, but if she didn't switch her tail, she would be good.

Last year, hunters had been trespassing on the land she normally ran on and shot at her, just missing her. Her shifter healing ability meant she healed in half the time that humans would heal, if she didn't bleed out first. But she didn't want to get shot on a cougar run ever. She had to find a hunter-free zone and she hoped the place she had found would be that for her. At least for a while until she could locate another such place. She was always afraid if anyone spied her, it would be all over the media. Rare white cougar spotted and then she'd have nowhere to run.

She finally reached the turnoff that she'd checked out before. It looked like an old road once used by wagons or maybe more modern vehicles but was overgrown now and it didn't look like anyone had used it in a long time. Her off-the-road, white Jeep Wrangler was perfect for it as she drove toward the barbed wire fence where she would park and strip and shift. She finally reached the fence and parked. She got out of her Jeep and stretched, loving the fall colors in Colorado, the aspens in their golden finery, the green firs in all their greenery, the blue spruce adding a majestic touch of silver blue to the landscape. A mountain of red rocks and boulders were a few hundred yards from the fence, and she was eager to jump up on the rocks clear to the top and see the panoramic vista.

Maybe she could even spy the waterfalls from there.

The air was chilly as she hurried to pull off her clothes, threw them in the Jeep, locked the keypad on her vehicle, and shifted. Then as a cougar she stretched again, eyeing the red cliffs she wanted to race up. She leaped over the old barbed-wire fence half dipping, the posts leaning over and then raced for the rocks. Signs were posted *No Trespassing, No Hunting,* but they didn't pertain to a cougar. With leaps and bounds, she finally reached the top of the rocks and sat up above, smelling the fresh air, seeing the pale glow of the crescent moon against the blue sky, whisps of clouds floating by.

It was just beautiful. She could sit up here all day and breathe in the fresh air and enjoy the fall chill in the air that didn't affect her as warm as her coat was.

From this vantage point, she saw a ranch way off in the distance. She hadn't been able to spy it from down below. She narrowed her eyes, looking to observe what she could see. Horses, maybe? Little dots moving around. Cows, maybe. It was a long way off.

Being a curious big cat, she wanted to learn if they were really horses or cows, and she wanted to see who all lived there. But she knew that ranchers wouldn't appreciate a cougar prowling around their ranch and their livestock and would shoot to kill. Not that she had any intention of hunting livestock. The *no tres-passing* signs would be meant for her then, and the *no hunting?* It didn't count when their livestock could be at risk.

A pickup truck pulled up near where she'd parked her vehicle, and her heart took a dive. What if whoever it was stole her vehicle? Or was the owner of the property having her vehicle towed for abandoning it? Police could be investigating who the vehicle belonged to. And if it was impounded, she'd be stuck here as a cougar without a stitch of clothes to wear!

"Hey, Sims, this looks like a prime hunting spot. But what about the other vehicle here?"

There was one thing she hated about fall. That hunters hunted and she was hunting game. Even if they were trespassing and not supposed to be hunting on the property.

Sims said, "Yeah, I recognize that vehicle. It belongs to one of the paralegals at the lawyer's office in Grand Junction where I had legal representation."

Omigod, Jeffrey Sims? He was a hulking six-foot-six brute and he looked like the kind of man who could be into a lot more illegal stuff than just trespassing and illegally hunting, though that was bad enough.

But his buddies, Clayton and Braxton, made an even more menacing trio—probably all thinking she was running around out here as a human.

"So? You think she's here to catch you illegally hunting?" The man snorted.

"Maybe she's hunting illegally too, Clayton. Wouldn't that be a hoot. She's out here trespassing like us, when her lawyer represented you on the hunting charges," Braxton said.

She recognized their voices from when they'd been in the lawyer's office.

"I don't see her, do you?" Sims asked.

"Hell, no, but look up there," Clayton said.

She'd already moved behind rocks to jump down the cliffs on the backside, but her darned tail was whipping about in a response to the mixture of frustration and anger she was feeling.

She wanted to bite the men, but not turn them, and that probably wouldn't fare well. They would be turned and then be rogue cougars, and she would have to terminate them. Which she didn't want to do. Then there would be a hunt for the killer cougar, and any puma would be on the hunters' hit list.

The men had already made it over or through the barbed-wire fence and were running around to the other side of the cliffs before she reached the bottom. One of the men fired a shot at her, the bullet hitting the cliff and splintering the rocks. Her heart skittered as she dodged through the rocks to the base, trying to find cover.

She considered leaping up the bare-faced cliffs again and over to the other side, clearing the fence, and returning to her vehicle.

But she was afraid they would wound her or kill her before she could make it. And climbing up the cliff would make her freely visible and the perfect moving target. Racing through the tall grasses was a better bet.

She could hear their heavy breathing and pounding boots on the ground some distance back.

"I'll be damned! A white cougar!" Clayton said.

"No way in hell. Shoot it!" Sims said.

Why would anyone want to kill a rare white cougar? Asses. Then a shot rang out and she felt a nip in her shoulder. Damn it. She'd been hit. She stumbled. Somehow, she had to swing on back to reach her car, dress, and get out of here. But who could take care of the bullet wound now? The police would be called in to investigate a bullet wound. And that was only if she could make it to her car in time, shift, get into her car, lock it, dress, and tear out of there, and reach a hospital.

The men were coming around down below. Another shot was fired, and it hit her arm. The same arm. She was so pissed off she wanted to scream. A good cougar screech could curdle their blood. But she didn't want to alert them as to where she really was. And then she wanted to pounce on them and bite them. No running away in fear of her life, damn it!

She was running full out as a cougar though, the adrenaline surging through her veins in flight mode. All she could do was head this time for the ranch. She'd seen several outbuildings. Maybe one of them would provide her cover where she could hide until she could heal enough and then make her way back to her Jeep.

With her cougar shifters' faster healing abilities, she thought she might make it. Worst-case scenario, she would just shift in a shed and if anyone found her, they would discover a naked woman was all. No cougar. No rare white cougar to kill. A bleeding woman that someone could take care of. How would she explain the part of how she was naked? That was going to be more difficult to deal with.

Maybe someone would have left some clothes in one of the sheds and she could at least be partially dressed. She figured that would be wishful thinking.

She wasn't sure about going to one of the buildings off in the distance though as she slowed her pace and began sneaking through the tall grasses now like a predator on a hunt, trying to keep as low a profile as she could so the hunters wouldn't see her, instead of like a cat who was being hunted and running off, trying to leave the danger behind.

"Where is she?" one of the hunters asked as they were still looking around the rocks.

Far away from you, she wanted to say, and she was glad they hadn't discovered she'd moved far away from the rocks.

"Watch for her. She's wounded and will be more dangerous," Sims said.

"She has run this way," Clayton said. "You can see where she has trampled down the grass some and it hasn't sprung back up. And there's some blood on the grass here."

Damn, at least one of the men was a good tracker. She wanted to sprint, run as fast as she could again to reach the buildings so she could hide. She was moving too slowly while trying to keep a low profile. The pain in her shoulder and arm hadn't kicked in yet at least.

Then Stella heard the rattle of a snake's tail, a big one as many rattles as she heard. For a split second, she was torn between leaping out of its way or avoiding jumping above the tall grasses she was navigating to keep out of the line of sight from the hunters. She didn't react fast enough, and the rattlesnake struck her in the back leg, damn it. Her heart was already racing, slow it down! She could imagine the poison pumping through her blood faster.

She was batting zero. She knew she needed to lie down and

stop the poison from speeding through her blood, but she also knew that she needed to stop the blood loss from the bullet wounds. Her only chance was hiding in the red barn, the outbuilding closest to where she was running. She could even cry out for help, once she shifted.

Immediately, the snake's bite on her hindleg began burning. *Great. Just great.*

She smelled the scent of horses ahead, but she realized she hadn't smelled the scent of the men behind her even when they had circled around her and she had outmaneuvered them. If they were wearing hunters' concealment, even if the wind direction was right for her to smell them, she wouldn't be able to. She came to the end of the tall grasses and found a pasture where the horses had been grazing and that meant *short* grass. She hadn't figured that into her plans.

A large red barn was closest to her location and both barn doors were wide open, offering her refuge from the hunters. Her heart was pounding in her ears, and she knew she had to make a mad dash for it. She saw a couple of beautiful Australian shepherds off in the distance, chasing each other around the ranch. Some guard dogs, but at least that was a good thing for her, and they were cute. She loved dogs.

Focus, Stella!

Hopefully, the dogs wouldn't see her at the last minute. She planned to hide, heal, and leave when it was pitch black out—if she could survive that long if she couldn't shift back to her human form—return to her vehicle as a cougar and get out of there. So much for this being a safe place to run as a cougar.

* * *

TED WEEKUM WAS busy showing his triplet brother, Bill, younger by five minutes, and an FBI agent, around the horse ranch Hal and Tracey Haverton owned out of Yuma Town, Colorado.

Tracey was out with her four-year old quadruplets setting up more Halloween and fall decorations, though he told her if she needed help with anything heavy, to let him know and he would take care of it. They'd been decorating all week because of the Halloween party they were having here at the end of next week. All suited up and looking distinguished, Larry Pierce was talking to her, their new lawyer in town, leaving a successful practice in Denver behind, wanting to join his only family, Yvonne Mueller, his sister, and Rick, his brother-in-law. Larry had been in an all-human practice before. They'd needed their own lawyer in Yuma Town to make up wills, take care of estate planning, and anything else that folks in the area needed legal counsel for. He'd just made up some sales contracts for Tracey and her mate for the sale of a couple of their horses. Larry had his leather briefcase in hand and was just saying goodbye to Tracey before he returned to town. Everyone loved that the lawyer was great about making house calls even! He was truly enjoying being here with a whole town of cougars.

"So what kind of FBI cases have you been working on?" Ted asked Bill. He thoroughly enjoyed visiting with his twin brother, though with Bill's FBI work and helping their sister to run a quarter horse ranch out of West Texas, Ted didn't get to see him very often.

Ted was glad his brother had come out to visit. Ted usually was the one to return home to visit since they lived in the Panhandle of Texas—his sister and his niece, and her two children. And his nephew had just mated, so he had them to see too. And Bill, unless he was on a big FBI case, was always there too.

But for Halloween, this was the place to be. Bill had spent several days even helping with decorations for the big party, though he wasn't staying for it.

Bill had his thumbs hooked in his belt loops and said, "We had to track down a horse theft ring. They put me in charge of the case because I help our sister run the ranch."

"Sounds like a good thing. Did you catch them?"

"Yeah. And we were able to rescue all the horses. Good thing too because they weren't taking care of them. They were just looking for a new buyer for them when the first buyer backed out of the deal."

"Why?"

"The horse thieves killed a ranch hand while stealing the horses, and that wasn't part of the deal. We caught the original buyer, who had traded in horseflesh before. And he told us who he thought was buying the horses and where they might be holding them so we wouldn't look into what he was up to these days. We were too busy trying to apprehend the murderers."

"Good thing you got them then."

Ted was going home to see his mom and sister and her kids for Thanksgiving this year. And he knew his sister would ask the question she always asked. When was he finding a mate, and why couldn't he work for her at her ranch instead of in Colorado? But Hal had hired him after he had worked as a ranch hand at another Colorado ranch when he couldn't work with his dad at all in Texas. His dad was dead, but Ted had been a foreman at the Haverton's ranch for several years now and enjoyed the work, and the people he worked with. Not to mention the whole town was cougar run, so he had a lot of cougar friends here.

As to finding a mate, he would have much better success at finding one here and not in West Texas. Even his niece was having trouble finding a new mate, though having a couple of boys, aged five and seven, didn't help either.

"When are you going to retire from the FBI and take over as foreman of the ranch?" Ted asked Bill.

"A few more years. Though that may change if I meet a pretty cougar."

Ted smiled. "Yeah, I know what you mean. Then you'll want to settle down and start having kids."

"I don't know about the kids' part, but I wouldn't mind

finding a filly of my own. I thought you would be mated by now. You've got several choices here."

"Nah. I mean, yeah, I've dated some, but I haven't found anyone that I'm ready to settle down with yet." Ted knew his brother would build a house on the ranch in Texas if he settled down with a she-cat then and have a home near their sister's place.

Out of the corner of Ted's eye, he thought he saw a flash of white. A shot was fired from a hunting rifle. Then another. He saw hunters then, three of them running through the tall grass, headed straight toward one of the red barns on the acreage, all three in camo gear, two with longish hair, the third man's hair cut short, military style.

"Damn it to hell," Ted said, racing to get his rifle, his heart drumming.

Bill had his gun out. He was always armed. Now Ted was glad he was, if anyone ever came after Bill because of an FBI case he'd been working on. "Hold it there! FBI agent!"

"Get the kids inside, Tracey!" Ted shouted.

Larry had a gift of gab and was still talking to Tracey when the shooting began. He dropped his briefcase and grabbed up the two boys, one under each arm and ran for the house. Tracey was already grabbing the two girls' hands and rushing the crying, terrified kids to the house while she shouted for the dogs, "Zula! Koda! Come!" She was a U.S. Fish and Wildlife Services special agent and could arrest the men, or Bill could. Ted knew she would be calling her mate too, who was a part-time deputy sheriff of Yuma Town also, working on a car theft case right now.

In fact, everyone from the sheriff's department, and the Cougar Special Forces special agents, would be here as soon as they could, once they heard about this.

Ted was glad Tracey had thought to take the dogs in the house. They had looked back at him to see if it was all right, and he had quickly motioned with his hand to command them to stay

11

with the kids and their mom and Larry. The dogs were all shook up because they knew Ted and Bill were riled up and the kids were crying, so they hadn't known who to stay with.

"They're shooting at the barn," Bill shouted, then called out to the hunters, again, pulling his badge out this time, "FBI agent. Drop your weapons. Hands in the air."

"No way in hell, man," one of the men shouted, as if it was all right for them to be shooting up private property in pursuit of their prey, when it was illegal as hell.

Ted was running with his rifle to join his brother and leveled his weapon at them. "Do as the agent says, now!"

"Listen, we're tracking a wounded white cougar and we're doing you a big damn favor by killing it for you," the one hunter said.

"Down on the ground now!" Bill said again.

"Hell, they want the white cougar for their own," the one man said and spit on the ground.

Ted frowned. Was that the white flash of something he had seen out of his peripheral vision? But he was damned concerned that the cougar was so gravely injured, he might die on them. He thought the men had to be mistaken. Ted had never seen a white cougar in his life. Never even heard of one either. But was the cougar they shot a shifter or a wild cougar?

Tracey came out of the house, her gun and badge in hand. "I'm a special agent with the Wildlife Service. You picked the wrong property to shoot up while hunting illegally on our property and trespassing. Do as the FBI agent said. Put your weapons down and put your hands up." Without taking her gaze off the men, she said to Ted and Bill, "I've notified the sheriff and everyone's on their way. CSF special agents also." Though she didn't say what that stood for. Humans didn't have a clue, but the CSF special agents took down hunters who illegally shot cougars, and rogue cougars who were on their terminal list for crimes they'd committed. They couldn't go to jail. Not when they could shift into a big bad cougar in a jail cell.

"Hell," one of the men said, and carefully put his rifle down. He must have been the leader of the band because the others did the same thing.

"Move away from the rifles," Ted said, meaning to let Tracey or Bill say it since they had more authority. He had to get to the wounded cougar though at once.

And they had to get these men away from here. The problem was that the ranch was a way out from town. Tracey moved to Bill and handed him zip ties to confine the men. Ted knew she had to get back inside to her kids who were probably scared to pieces about what was going on. Their nanny had gone into town to buy groceries for Tracey.

Just then, Kolby, their other ranch hand came around the barn carrying a rope and his mouth gaped.

Ted turned to him and said for his ears only, "Go get a first aid kit from the bunkhouse. We've got a wounded cougar in the barn if these men are right and they haven't killed him."

"Yes, sir." Kolby dropped the rope and raced off.

Ted kept his rifle trained on the men while Bill zip tied their wrists.

Then Kolby returned with the first aid kit and handed it to Ted.

"Call the vet," Ted said as an afterthought.

"I already did."

"Good." Then Ted handed Kolby the rifle to watch the men. The kid was bright and had been a real welcome addition to the staff at the ranch.

Tracey said, "I'll be right back. Shoot them if they try to get away." She smiled at Bill, but it was more sinister than sweet and then she ducked inside.

Ted ran toward the building, and inside, he immediately

smelled the scent of a female cougar and fresh blood—presumably hers.

"Hell, man, do you want to get yourself killed? We told you it's wounded," one of the shooters said.

"No thanks to you." Ted shut the barn doors. The darkness didn't bother him. He could see well enough as a cougar at night. But he did worry that the cougar might be just a cougar. He couldn't take the chance that it would die on him before he checked her out though, if she was a shifter like they were. "I'm Ted Weekum, a cougar shifter, so if you're one too, you don't have to worry about my intentions. I'm the foreman for the horse ranch and all of us working here and in Yuma Town are cougars. I've got a first aid kit so I can take care of you until the vet comes. She's a cougar also. The men who shot you are human and are being taken into custody. You won't have to see them again. They'll be up on charges for shooting up the property and endangering the people on the ranch."

He peered around the place. "If you don't believe me, I can strip and shift for you. Anything to reassure you were the good guys." That was if the cougar was a shifter like them. Otherwise, there was a big cat reserve he would take her to, once she was healed up and it was safe to leave her at the reserve.

* * *

STELLA GROANED as she lifted her head, her shoulder and her arm hurting like the devil, her leg where she'd been bitten by the rattler feeling numb and swollen. She wanted to shift, but when she hurt like this, it was like her brain short-circuited and she couldn't shift back. Which shot her whole plan to pieces because she had planned to turn into a human and then the men wouldn't shoot her. So if the man talking to her was a cougar shifter for real like her, then she was finally having a bit of luck.

She heard sirens in the distance, and she'd heard another man say that he was FBI and a woman say she was a special agent with the Fish and Wildlife Services outside the building Stella was hiding in. She knew that woman would protect her. She hadn't been sure about the FBI agent who would have probably wanted to put her out of her misery, but if they were all cougar shifters, that was a whole different story.

She snarled at Ted to let him know she was up in the loft, hiding behind some stacks of hay.

The police cars pulled close to the house, and then there were others shouting orders as Ted climbed the ladder to reach her. She was hoping her snarl hadn't sounded angry, but she couldn't seem to make any sound other than a hurt, growly one.

When he reached the top, he peered into the gloom, a little light coming through a few slats of wood and she saw a dark-haired man with blue eyes, and a concerned expression furrowing his brow. He was wearing a light-colored Stetson, a blue plaid western shirt, well-worn jeans, and a pair of scuffed-up cowboy boots. He looked like a real cowboy. If she wasn't so injured, she would have smiled at the sight. He would make for the perfect, handsome cowboy in a historical western. Well, or a modern cowboy. Yeah, riding the ranges, corralling cattle, and coming to take her out on a date. Maybe even teach her to ride a horse. But she wasn't sure he would be interested in a woman who couldn't ride a horse.

"Can you shift? It would be easier to bandage you," Ted said.

She wanted to shift. She wanted to tell him she had been bitten by a rattlesnake. Though when she'd had a German shepherd as a kid and the vet had told her mother that they didn't need to do anything, the dog would recover. Except they had to keep it calm, not like what she'd been doing, running to the barn. But now? She wasn't going to move a muscle. She was desperately trying to shift, but sometimes when wounded, injured, or sick a shifter couldn't easily shift from one form to another. This appeared to be one of those times and she should have thought of that too. She guessed she'd been too panicked to think clearly when she had been trying to find a safe spot to hide.

"Are you injured anywhere else?" Ted pulled bandages out of the first aid kit.

He was lucky she wasn't all cougar.

"Your shoulder," he said, answering himself since she couldn't. "And your arm. I'm going to apply a bandage to each wound to stop the bleeding. Dr. Vanessa Rugel should be here soon." He worked on her as gently as he could, but the pain was hitting all at once and she snarled at him because it hurt, and she instantly felt guilty. He was only trying to save her life. "Sorry. Do you have any other injuries?"

She lifted her hind leg a little and he went back to check on it. "Well, damn. The area on your leg is swollen, but there's no blood from a bullet wound. Were you bitten by a rattlesnake? It has to be a snakebite. We'll have to get you an antidote. As a cougar, you'll be okay, staying quiet, but if you shift—we need to get you an antidote no matter what." He got on his phone and said, "Our cougar had been bitten by a snake." He glanced down at Stella. "Rattlesnake?"

She nodded.

"Yeah, rattlesnake," he told the vet.

"Okay, thanks." He ended the call and said to Stella, "The veterinarian, Vanessa Rugel, is calling someone at her animal clinic to pick up the antidote. She's already on her way here. She's going to patch you up before she takes you to the clinic. If you can hold off, don't shift until you have the antidote for the poison in your blood."

Then they heard another vehicle pull up. "That's the vet," Ted said.

Stella wanted to thank him and everyone else for taking care of her.

Then she heard the doors open to the barn and she was afraid for her life all over again. That the hunters got loose somehow and were going to shoot her for good.

But someone outside was reading the men their Miranda rights, and then loading them up in a couple of cars.

"I've got one of them, Dan," one man said.

"I'll take that one, Dan," another man said.

"I'll take the last one. You stay here, Hal. Your mate will probably be shook up, or at least the kids will be. And, Ricky, if you need to be here for the family since you worked for them for so long as a ranch hand, you're welcome to stay."

"Thanks, Dan," one of the men said. "I'll go in and check on Tracey and the kids." So that had to be Hal.

Then three cars took off and another drove into the parking area while two men entered the barn.

"What did you find?" one of the men asked.

"An injured female cougar, a rare white, and I assume she's one of us, Bill. That's my brother Bill," Ted said for Stella's benefit.

She finally managed to lick Ted's hand and he smiled at her.

"Can I see her?" another man asked.

"That's Kolby Jones, one of our ranch hands."

"Me too," another man said, that sounded similar to the first.

"Ricky Jones, his brother, a deputy sheriff now, but he used to be one of our ranch hands."

Bill said, "The vet's here."

"Once she sees to her, we can carry her down. I think she's in too much pain to shift," Ted said.

The woman came into the barn. "Where is the cougar?"

"Up here in the loft," Ted said.

"I don't usually climb into lofts to see my patients, but there's always a first time for everything." When the vet reached the loft, she said, "I'm Dr. Vanessa Rugel. We'll get you to the clinic right away."

She checked her heart rate and pulse. She gave her a shot for the pain and Stella felt like she was drifting on clouds. She still felt the pain, but it was duller, farther away, as if she could distance herself from it. Then the veterinarian climbed down the ladder from the loft so the guys could rig up something to carry Stella in and lower her down to the ground. Once they had moved her, they lifted her onto a stretcher and carried her out to a waiting ambulance.

Before the ambulance pulled out, another vehicle raced into the yard, a car door opened, and feet hit gravel. The doctor said, "Thanks!"

Then Stella felt a swipe of a piece of sterile cloth covered in the smell of alcohol and cold and wet against her skin, a sharp jab of a needle after that, and a liquid pouring into her body.

"It's the antivenom," the doctor said, "and it will take care of the poison in your blood."

Stella felt relief, hoping they'd caught the poison in time and counteracted it.

"If they don't get these guys on criminal charges, I'll file a civil suit on your behalf," a suited man said, moving in to speak to her, his kindly blue eyes looking down at her, his hand on her furry cougar head. "They won't get away with it."

"He's our town's lawyer," Ted said. "Larry Pierce."

Ambulance chaser, Stella thought. She was drifting even more now, but she was surprised she was going for a ride in an ambulance. She figured she would be in a cage in a truck bed or something, but this was nice.

The next thing she vaguely remembered was being carried into an animal clinic and then she was out.

CHAPTER 2

*T*ed had a job to do here at the ranch, otherwise he wanted to check on the cougar. He told himself it was because he had taken care of her first. But it was more than that. He had to have closure, and he was praying she would make it through surgery all right. But his place was here at the ranch. He still had blood on his hands from when he had bandaged her to try and stop the bleeding. And some on his clothes even. He hoped she hadn't lost too much blood.

He hurried to wash the blood off his hands outside at the spigot.

Tracey was on her cell while Hal was watching the kids. "Okay, Vanessa." She glanced at Ted and Bill. "Do either of you have O negative blood?"

"I do," Bill and Ted said at the same time.

"Vanessa needs you to donate blood."

Ted was already headed for his pickup. Bill was going with him. "Probably only one of us needs to give her blood," Ted said to his brother.

"Yeah, I was thinking the same." But from the way he spoke the words, Bill intended to be the one who gave her his blood.

"I guess she can't have too much blood, if Vanessa needs more," Ted said.

"Right." Bill gave him a quirky smile as Ted drove them off the ranch.

They drove in silence for a while, then Bill said, "She might be too old for us."

Ted cast him an annoyed look. "She might be mated or seeing someone. What has that got to do with anything?"

"She probably didn't run here from miles away. Those hunters were on foot. They must have been nearby too."

Ted frowned, then snapped his fingers. "Vehicles. They've left their vehicles somewhere nearby."

"Right. Somewhere they could park and then access the property without being seen."

"Off the main road, there's an old turnout. It used to be a road through the property—old dirt road, once even used by wagons. But the road running through the property from that direction has been fenced off for ages." Ted got on his phone and called Tracey. "Hey, Bill had an idea. The hunters, and the cougar, probably parked somewhere close by. Maybe on the old wagon road."

"We'll check it out and if we find a couple of vehicles there, we'll confiscate them," Tracey said.

Ted smiled.

"Thanks, Ted, Bill. I told Vanessa you're both on your way," Tracey said.

"How badly wounded is the cougar?" Ted asked.

"Bad enough to need a blood transfusion. She must have run some distance while she was bleeding with no pressure to stop it. I'm calling Dan to see if I can get some backup to look for the cars. Kolby's got babysitting duty and Hal's going with me, but we'll need a couple of tow trucks too once we find them. Dan's booked the men and they're all sitting in jail for now because of shooting at the property when the kids and I were out and could have been hit by the bullets. Same with you all."

"Okay, good. Let us know what happens."

"We will. Once we find the vehicles, we'll be able to verify license plates and who owns them and then hopefully learn who the woman is."

"All right, thanks." Then Ted ended the call with Tracey.

"Here I thought the business *I* did could be dangerous," Bill said.

"When hunters want something, there's no telling how dangerous some of them can be. Most are fine, obey the laws, and don't cause trouble. But then you've got a few bad eggs who ruin it for the rest," Ted said.

When they finally reached the animal clinic, Ted knew the woman would get the best of care. One of the beds was set up like a human bed, so that if a cougar was injured as a cougar, when the person shifted, he or she would be on a human-sized bed. They had the same for the surgery ward in the event the shifter turned into their human form during the surgery and they would be too large for a standard pet surgery table.

"Is she all right?" Ted asked Pamela Lang, the receptionist. "We're here to donate blood."

"I'll call right back." Pamela called to one of the rooms in the back.

Riley Manning, one of the vet techs, hurried out to usher them back to give blood. "You've got to strip and shift. She's still a cougar and we need cougar blood."

As soon as Ted and Bill had stripped off their clothes, they shifted and hopped up on tables where they laid down to give blood—something they normally didn't have to do. One shifter, maybe, but not two. Ted again hoped the woman would be all right. But he was thinking, if she shifted during the surgery, or before, he and his brother would have to give human blood.

Vanessa came into the room in a hurry. "No, no, one has to give human blood in case she needs it."

"Sorry," Riley said. "Hey, Ted, if you can shift back, I'll take blood from you then." He'd already started the IV on Bill who was in his cougar form.

Ted shifted and tugged on his boxer briefs, but he wouldn't fit on the animal table to give blood now. They had him sit in a chair that could be leaned back, then started the IV on him. He smiled at his brother. "This is one time that I can say things to you, and you can't talk back."

His brother gave him a toothy grin.

Ted really wanted to know what was going on with the woman—and learn who she was—not in a way that meant he wanted to date her. What if she had family? They had to let them know what had happened to her.

She appeared to be about thirty or so and he and his brother were thirty-three, so the right age for dating, though. Okay, so he was interested. He was fascinated by the fact she was a white cougar. He could just imagine all the kids in Yuma Town wanting to see her for show and tell. Poor cougar.

Then he finally finished giving blood and Riley gave him orange juice to drink. Once Ted had finished that, he had to sit for a few minutes, to make sure he wouldn't pass out from giving blood, though his own blood supply would build back up faster than a human's would.

His brother had finished giving blood and looked a little sleepy. He wasn't shifting back either. That's all he needed to do was shift and pass out.

"I've got an orange juice for you too, when you shift," Riley said to Bill.

Bill opened his eyes and nodded. He was strapped to the table so he wouldn't fall off if giving blood had made him feel woozy.

Then the vet tech left with the blood and Ted waited until he was done waiting, got up, and started to pull on his jeans. But the next thing he knew, the whole world was shifting, tilting, half of it turning black and then all of it dissolved in blackness.

"Ted! Ted!" he heard Dr. Vanessa calling from far away and he looked up at her, feeling a killer headache coming on and his stomach was revolting.

"You weren't supposed to move from the chair until I said so," Vanessa said, looking down sternly at him as she applied a bandage to his head.

"What...?" Ted felt disoriented, unsure as to what had happened, realizing he was lying on the cold, linoleum floor.

"You got up too quickly after giving blood, passed out, and hit your head on the edge of the counter. You'll have a goose's egg, bruising, and you had a cut, but not bad enough to require stitches. We're going to help you up, but you have to sit in the chair until I tell you that you can move." Vanessa was part stern, part concerned. She told Riley, "Next time we have one of our shifters donating human blood, strap him or her in too." She shook her head, then she pulled off Ted's jeans still resting at his ankles.

She and Riley lifted him up and he couldn't believe how unsteady he was on his feet. Then they helped him into the chair. Ted couldn't have been more furious about what had gone down at the ranch. But he'd been just as angry at himself for injuring himself just because he was so damned impatient to see the cougar who'd been shot, once he realized what had happened to him.

"Can we rely on you to stay put?" Doc asked, looking worried again.

He let out his breath in exasperation. "Yes, ma'am."

"Good. Stella White is out of surgery and in recovery. They found her vehicle and towed it into the sheriff's department's compound along with the hunters' pickup. We know who she is now, but she's still out of it, really groggy."

"Oh, okay. It's good that she's going to be okay, right?"

"Hopefully. We won't know until she comes out of the recovery room completely. She's still in her cougar form."

Bill had been sleeping, apparently, and now was lying on his table as a human, legs hanging over the end of the table, a blanket over him and a pillow under his head. He was watching Ted, a silly smirk splitting his face.

He'd probably seen what had happened to Ted, or maybe he'd only seen the end result.

When Vanessa and the technician left, Bill shook his head. "You always try to rush things."

Ted scoffed. "As if you wouldn't? You were strapped down as a cougar or you would have done the same thing as me." Ted knew his brother well enough to know he would have too.

Bill only smiled. "Okay, you're probably right. I would hope I would have been more graceful about it. Just so you know, I called for help as soon as you began pulling on your jeans and then threw out your arms as if you were trying to stop yourself from falling. And not in a way that said you were losing your balance, but that you were passing out. You know it's hard to cry out as a cougar when I wanted to yell for help as a human. I even considered shifting, but I was afraid I would do the same thing, and no one would come to assist you."

"I felt fine, just a little dizzy when I rose too quickly, but then I thought I would overcome it."

Family physician Dr. William Rugel came into the room, folded his arms, and looked crossly at Ted.

Ted smiled. "Hey, Doc, what brings you here?"

"I came to check on Vanessa's other patient, but then here you were injuring yourself, so she asked me to step in and take a look at you."

"Is Stella in her human form now?" Ted asked, eager to see her.

"Yeah, she is, which is why I've come to see her."

And his mate, Vanessa, Ted figured. They took every chance they could to see each other as newly mated cougars. Sure, they mated last year, but that still counted as newly mated.

William flashed a light in Ted's eyes and checked over the head wound. "You should be checked over for a concussion."

"I'm fine," Ted said.

His brother was smiling, getting too much of a kick out of this.

"We'll see what Hal wants done," William said.

"Hal? It's my damn head. And he knows how hard it is."

"That's for damn sure," Bill said.

"I'm having it okayed by him because you work for him and he's not going to want you to work at some of the heavy lifting or other chores you do on the ranch until he knows for sure you're all right to finally return to work." Doc got on his phone and said, "Hey, Hal, I'm seeing Ted now. I think he needs an MRI just to make sure he's all right...yes, I will." He smiled. "Right. I'll tell him." Then Doc called another number. "Yeah, have the ambulance brought over to the animal clinic. We're taking a patient to the clinic to have an MRI done. Ted Weekum." Doc looked up at him. "Yeah, he's agreeing to it, per his boss's and *my* orders."

Bill said, "I'll tell Stella you want to see her as soon as she comes out of recovery."

Yeah, if the cougar was single and lived around the area, Bill was making a move on her. She better not think Bill was the one who had helped her when she'd been wounded, as similar as he and his brother looked.

CHAPTER 3

*S*tella finally had more of a clear head and realized she
was dressed in a clinic gown and lying under a blanket
of white. She was in…she glanced around at all the pictures on
the walls—an animal clinic, pictures of dogs and cats featured on
the walls everywhere. And there were even a few plant-eating
dinosaurs, that she smiled about. A brachiosaurus and a bron-
tosaurus. Even Halloween decorations of pumpkins and black
cats.

She was surprised to see a regular clinic bed here, but then
recalled what Ted Weekum had told her about the place being
cougar shifter held territory, and that the vet was a cougar too.

A man entered the room and said he was Dr. William Rugel.
"I'm having you transferred to the clinic. I'm a family physician
and my mate, Vanessa, took care of you when you were in your
cougar form. She'll come by to see you off, but she did an excellent job of removing both bullets and you should be good unless
you end up with an infection. She also gave you an antivenom for
the rattlesnake bite while you were still a cougar to counteract
the poison as quickly as possible. We'll keep you at the clinic for a

couple of days to ensure you'll be fine for the gunshot wounds and the rattlesnake bite."

"How did she know it was a rattlesnake bite? Oh, Ted asked me, and I nodded my head. Okay. What if I accidentally shift into the cougar?" She was afraid she would cause the clinic real trouble then.

"We have a couple of patient rooms for cougars only. We send patients who are strictly human off to other clinics once they're stabilized if they come to us with health emergencies. You'll be safe."

What a great deal that was. "Oh. Okay, thanks."

Then Vanessa came into the room and Stella vaguely remembered seeing her before the drugs had knocked her out.

"You're in good shape to leave," Vanessa said. "I have to tell you right now, the bachelor cougars of Yuma Cougar will want to know if you're single or not, even if you have no intention of living around here."

Stella chuckled. She couldn't believe being shot and bitten by a rattlesnake, then hiding out at a horse ranch might lead to a date with a cougar. "I'm single, but I'm a paralegal for a law firm in Grand Junction, Colorado. So I don't have any plan to leave the job."

"Okay, I'll let anyone know who asks."

"Like me," a man said who looked similarly to the man who had bandaged her in the barn. But he...didn't smell the same.

"I'm Bill Weekum. But I live in West Texas normally. I'm just visiting Ted, my brother."

"Ted..." she said softly under her breath.

"Looks like a lost cause for me," Bill said. "I'm glad to see you awake and alert. My brother had to be taken to the clinic for an MRI, but I'm sure once he learns you're over there, he'll want to see you for himself."

"Did they catch the hunters?" She immediately worried they were still running loose and ready to shoot other cougars.

"They did. They charged them and put them in jail. Your vehicle and theirs have been impounded. They did that with your vehicle so it wouldn't be vandalized or stolen. You're free to go as soon as you're healed up enough."

"One of the men is named Jeffrey Sims. He was caught trespassing and shot wildlife on another ranch owner's property, but one of the lawyers I work for got him off," Stella said.

"Okay, we'll check into that further. I think we can get the charges to stick this time." Then Bill snapped his fingers. "They shot you. A human."

She frowned at him. "They shot me as a cougar."

"You were in the barn and they fired through the walls of the building. We have holes all over the place. If you hadn't been hiding behind the stacks of hay in the hayloft way up above, they might have killed you. But they were aiming lower where they thought the cougar was down below. They were too afraid to go in and confront you first, instead, shooting up the building, hoping to kill you that way," Bill said.

"Then that's it. I didn't see them, but their bullets were in me so that proves they shot me. They can't say they only shot a cougar."

"Exactly," Bill said.

Then the ambulance returned to the animal clinic to transport Stella to the clinic and all she could think of was what had happened to Ted? Had he been shot by the hunters while trying to protect her? All kinds of scenarios were rushing through her mind and she should have asked Bill first thing about him! She'd been so worried about the hunters still shooting all over the place at the ranch.

Bill said he'd see her at the clinic in a little while and while she was in the ambulance on the ride over there, she asked the EMT, "What happened to Ted?"

"He rose too quickly from the chair where he was sitting after he'd given blood and passed out. He'd hit his head pretty hard."

"For me? He'd given blood for me?"

"Yes. I'm sure he'll be all right, but he's going to have a goose egg and be black and blue for a while."

"Thanks for telling me."

"I didn't want you to believe it was something worse. His boss, Hal Haverton, wanted him checked out before he returned to work. Hal didn't want Ted further injuring himself while performing duties at the horse ranch."

"Ted's a foreman."

"Yes."

They finally reached the clinic, and she was taken inside on the gurney. The man she'd seen before, the real Ted, was just coming out of a room and gave her a big smile when he saw her, a bandage on his temple. Then he looked worried. "Are you all right?"

She scoffed. "I probably look better than you do now."

He smiled at her again.

Then they wheeled her into a room, and he came in to help them move her to a bed.

Once she was settled, the nurse, Elsie Miller, wearing pumpkin and ghost scrubs came in to take her vital signs, but Ted didn't leave.

"So you're not from around here," Ted said.

"I think that would be obvious, especially from the white fur coat I wear."

"Yeah. That's pretty special."

She sighed. "Unless you're so rare hunters want to kill you to show your pelt off."

"All the kids in Yuma Town and the surrounding areas want to see you. No picture taking as we don't want the word to spread that we have a rare white cougar out here. But probably none of us have seen one, so if you're agreeable, when you're on your feet again, could you shift and show them?"

"A great science project, like show and tell."

He chuckled. "Yeah, I guess. They may never see another one in their lifetime." Elsie had left, and he said, "If you want me to sneak anything into you that they might not have on the menu for dinner—"

Dr. Kate Parker Hill walked into the room, shaking her head at him. "You will be banned from the clinic during Stella's stay *after* you leave here." She gave him a sweet smile.

He laughed. "Well, I'm sure all their food will be great."

"I'm so glad you think so because you're staying overnight," Kate said.

"No way in hell."

Stella smiled at the cougar. He looked like he could wrangle horses with finesse, lift hefty bales of hay, and she thought he was cute in his western wear. She'd always had a thing for westerns and cowboys. A cowboy that was also a cougar? Now what a great combination. But she noticed he had blood on his plaid shirt and wondered if that was *her* blood.

"Yes, way. Doc William and I looked over the MRI and we both agree it's prudent for you to stay overnight. So no outside food for you either," Kate said.

Then Ted's growly expression brightened. "Can I share a room with a fellow patient?"

"It's up to the patient in question," Kate said.

Ted looked so hopeful Stella would agree, she smiled and nodded. She wanted to know more about this town that was cougar run. But while he was stripping and climbing into a clinic gown behind a curtain, appearing eager to room with her tonight, she fell asleep.

* * *

"Now, let her get her rest," Doc told Ted as he laid down on the bed and she covered him with the blanket.

He fully intended to once he and Stella talked a bit. But when Kate pulled the curtain aside, he saw Stella had rolled onto her side, facing him, and was sound asleep.

"Let her sleep," Doc said softly, reiterating her orders.

He knew Dr. Kate would move him out of the room in a heartbeat if he disobeyed her.

Besides, he was feeling tired himself, the headache still plaguing him.

Not that he'd planned to tell Kate or William about it. And he'd tried not to wince or show in any way that it was troubling him. He knew it would go away on its own. He must have slept for a while when he heard his brother talking low to someone nearby. His eyes shot open.

Bill. He had come to speak to Stella. The only good thing about that was that he lived so far away, Ted didn't think Bill could convince her to leave Colorado and join him in Texas, but who knew?

"Hey, how are you doing, Stella?" Bill asked her.

"I'm doing better, thanks." Then Stella glanced over at Ted and her expressive blue-green eyes widened. But then she smiled. "I'm sorry. Did we wake you?"

"No, I didn't expect to sleep at all. Did you bring us dinner?" he asked his brother.

Bill laughed. "Kate read me the riot act. You eat what they have here for dinner tonight. Hopefully, you will be back at work tomorrow. I can check on Stella."

Hell, now Ted didn't want to be released to return to work and that had never happened to him, ever. He loved his job and the Haverton family was like his own.

Kolby came into the room and smiled broadly at Stella, bringing her red roses.

Why hadn't Ted thought of that? But neither had Bill. Then Elsie came into the room and set vases of more roses on the table near Stella's bed. "I'm sure you'll get lots more." Then Elsie smiled and left the room.

Stella smiled as she read the card. "Thanks, Bill and Ted."

Ahh, hell, Ted wanted to get her his *own* flowers!

"And thanks—" Stella said to Kolby.

"Kolby is the name. I'm a ranch hand at the Haverton's ranch, ma'am. I helped capture the men who shot you." He was all smiles.

Ted wanted to tell Kolby to look for someone his own age.

Then the food was served, and Bill said, "Okay, I'm off to have dinner with the Havertons. See you when they release you, Ted. Good night, Stella. Sleep well." Bill was about to leave when he noticed Kolby was hanging around. "Come on, Kolby. You'll make everyone wait on dinner when you know they want to put the kids to bed."

Then Bill and Kolby left, and Ted and Stella were alone, and Ted was blissfully grateful.

"So tell me something about your family." Ted wanted to get to know Stella and that meant getting to know her family too.

"Truthfully, I don't have anything to do with my birth parents. My dad thought there was something wrong with my mom because I was a white cougar when I was born," Stella explained, running her hands over the white clinic blanket. "As I got older, he acted worse about me having white fur and wouldn't let me run at all as a cougar, believing I would shame the family if any other cougar shifters saw me like that."

"Hell, it could have been *his* genes that produced your beautiful white fur." Ted already knew he wouldn't like her dad.

"Yeah, exactly. Except he didn't see it that way. Mom always told me she loved me, but I could tell she was torn between loving me and loving my dad. As far as he was concerned, he couldn't love us both equally. She finally gave me up for adoption so she could stay with my dad and keep the peace."

Ted shook his head. He couldn't believe anyone would give up their only child to another family for no other reason than she had a different color of fur than her parents. Though his own dad had been abusive, and his mother stayed with his dad, so there were some similarities Ted and Stella had with regard to having family issues.

"Anyway, they never had any more kids, like they felt they were cursed because of me and might have more with white coats just like me. But my adoptive parents accepted me just fine. I think it was because they hadn't produced me. So they didn't feel any shame in that. Some cougars have looked at me differently once they learn of the color of my coat, so I've dated mostly humans. Being rare doesn't mean you're special. It means you're an oddity."

"I sure don't see you that way."

"Well, thanks. But everyone wants to see me because—"

"You're rare and special. It's a cougar run town. We're all special. We all care about each other. You won't find any negativism here. Maybe shock, surprise, astonishment, from those who haven't met you before. But they'll see how beautiful you are."

She sighed. "It has made me reject my kind. But when you came to help me, you were so kind and caring—even knowing upfront about the color of my fur, it made me realize not everyone is the same."

"No. Just like with my dad. He was really hard on me and I left home at sixteen. He finally died, but I couldn't go back. I'd made my home here. My mother didn't leave him either, but she protected us the best she could. My father was fine toward her and my sister. He just had a hard time dealing with my brother and me. I have to admit we did get in a fair amount of trouble when we were kids and teens. Nothing illegal, but just being reckless, adventurous, as cougars. My sister wasn't like that. My niece wasn't either, but she ended up with a bad mate. They're divorced now and she has two kids to raise. I think she's going to move back to the ranch house to help her mom with things."

"But you never want to return?"

"No. Not except for special occasions. My life is here. Bill's is in Texas. When he retires from the FBI, he'll take over the ranch. It's his and my sister's and I would never take that from them. Not when my brother goes home as much as he can to help out at the old homestead."

"So you'll remain the foreman at the Haverton's ranch."

"As long as they'll have me, yeah. So what happened to your adoptive parents?"

"They emancipated me at sixteen. Long story. They were good to me when I was little, and I really needed that in my life, but it was only because I did what they told me to do without question. But when I was a teen, I began to rail against some of the rules. Mainly, that I couldn't run as a cougar ever because of my white fur. So they would happily take their evening jaunts to run and I was forbidden to leave the house. They were going to move, and I actually liked the school I was attending, though most of us are homeschooled. But I proposed they emancipate me since I was not going with them, and they happily agreed. No fuss, no muss. I expected a big fight, or at least some discussion back and forth, but they were glad—at that point—to be rid of me. So I knew then that though they had said my white fur didn't matter, it did. I had to run, so when they were off on their jaunts, I went in the opposite direction and always timed myself so I would get home before they did."

Hell, Ted couldn't imagine not being able to run as a cougar when he was a teen.

"I think they never knew I'd been running on my own as a cougar. At least that was my thought on the matter, but as cougars? Who knows? They might have come across my cougar trails at some time and knew just what I had been up to. They never said anything, and I didn't either."

"Did they move with the intention of taking you out of that environment?"

She laughed. "No. They left articles around the house—the kitchen island, the coffee table—about teens emancipating themselves from their guardians—or else I would never have thought of it. I mean, at the time, I just thought it was by accident. But when they didn't object to my saying I wanted to be emancipated, and said they'd go along with it—even having encouraged me to get a job well before that so I could support myself—not well, but enough to get by and they'd send me money to help with my education until I was eighteen—so I figured it was their plan all along. It worked! And I was happily emancipated and no longer a threat to them when I ran as a cougar in the wild. Once I turned eighteen, they cut off support, though I could have used the help, and then I never heard from them again. I did check to see where they lived, but they had moved, leaving no forwarding address."

"Hell." He couldn't imagine being on his own at that age without a decent job and a roof over his head. The guys he worked with and the man he worked for were human, but at least they knew his family history and they had been there for him.

"It's no worse than your situation," Stella said.

"Only as far as I left home at sixteen to work on Bob Johnson's ranch, but at least as long as I worked hard, I had a roof over my head, food, a beat-up old pickup, a job, and pay. I can't imagine what you would have gone through."

"It was rough sometimes, but you know, I always had plans and I tried not to think about wishing for what I couldn't have—cougar friends who didn't see me as an oddity."

"We wouldn't treat you like that here."

She smiled.

"So what do you do?" he asked.

"I'm a paralegal for Brown and Sons. I like the job well enough. No cougars work there though. I wanted to find a place to run and I found this area and thought it would be safe."

"Hal and Tracey's property is safe, for the most part. But we have had hunters trespass before and they're fined heavily, sometimes with jail time. This time they'll get jail time because they were shooting at the property and they shot you and could have hit others, including the Haverton's four-year-old quadruplets and their mother."

Tears sprang into Stella's eyes. "Oh, God, I'm so sorry. I never thought they would shoot the ranch up. I only saw the outbuildings, no one there, just the dogs playing with each other. I just thought I could hide there and shift. If the hunters checked out the barn and found me, I would have been human, but then I couldn't shift and was afraid I was done for. Not just because of the trespassing hunters illegally hunting on the property, but whoever was managing the ranch would want me dead, afraid I would go after the horses. Explaining why I was a wounded human who was naked in your barn was one thing, but there was no explaining being a wounded cougar there. I did smell all the cougar scents in the place, but I just wasn't thinking clearly. At one point, I believed that the owners had killed cougars and stored them in there for a while. That wasn't reassuring.

"I'm glad you came to speak with me. I didn't trust you right away, until I smelled you were a shifter. I knew you wouldn't be talking to me and bandaging me up if you had wanted to harm me. But I still couldn't believe a whole community of cougars lived together either. It must be nice."

"Believe me, it is. We look out for each other." They finished their dinners and set their tables aside. "I would have gotten you flowers, if I hadn't been so out of it."

She smiled. "Your brother got them for me from the both of you. I figured as much, but that was sweet of him to include you too. I should have given flowers to *you* for coming to my aid and reassuring me I was in a safe place, and then giving me blood and injuring yourself afterward."

"Yeah, don't mention that part. Everyone will rib me about that forever."

She smiled. "How does your head feel?"

"Better, after I slept. The Havertons, or another family, will probably want to put you up for a couple of days before you leave, after the doctor releases you." Ted hoped she would agree to stay with them.

"We'll see. I need to get back to work on Monday. So if I'm stuck at the clinic for the weekend, I'll just return home, Sunday night, hopefully."

"Bill was telling me about Dan charging the men with shooting you when you were human."

"True."

"So you should be able to get off work for that. And the police reports are all done by our own cougars, so there will be no issues with that."

"Okay, good."

"I hear you're from Grand Junction."

"I am."

"You like to live dangerously."

She smiled. "I know. The place has the reputation of being dangerous there because of the number of both violent crimes and property crimes. That's why the law firm I work for does so well. They're always defending a number of criminal cases."

Ted shook his head. "Then the guilty get off for the crimes they were charged with."

"Well, you know they have to have the best legal representation to get a fair trial."

Then they both grew quiet. He was thinking of how he was going to see her again. He was always busy at the ranch, but Hal and Tracey would give him time off when he needed it. He was thinking he would have to visit Stella where she lived, to show her he still cared about what happened to her. He couldn't imagine living among strictly humans and not enjoying the time as a cougar with others like them. But some cougars were real loners and maybe she'd learned to live like that.

"So what do you do as a paralegal? I've never met one before," he said.

"I do a lot of research in my job, to determine the legality of the situation and all the facts in the case. I end up drafting court documents, review and summarize documents and file papers with the court. I communicate with the clients and maintain the files."

"It sounds to me like you do everything."

"No, I'm important to the support of the lawyer's case, but I'm not a lawyer. I love doing research and drafting up the court documents. Well, all of it really."

"That's good. And you haven't had any trouble with the crime in Grand Junction?"

"My apartment was broken into once. I really didn't have anything worth stealing. So they didn't get anything. I have my laptop at work with me, just in case anyone breaks into my apartment."

"You ought to live here. We deal with crime in a hurry, and so we rarely have trouble. A few rogue cougars, a few bad humans, but no one in the town causes us trouble."

"That sounds good." She'd never lived anywhere else than Grand Junction, born and raised.

"I'm glad you're here, despite the circumstances."

"I'm glad I am too." She felt bad that he had hurt himself after giving her blood. He seemed sweet and so was his brother. In fact everyone was so caring, it was refreshing. Particularly since they were all cougars. She was so unused to being around cougars, she wasn't even sure how she would interact with a whole town full of them. She guessed she'd been a loner for so long, she was used to it.

She was feeling tired again, glad she wasn't nauseous or having any numbness due to the snakebite. She figured they must have given her the antivenom quickly enough to counteract the poison.

"I would like to see you after you return home sometime," he said.

She smiled. "I would like that." Then she closed her eyes, too tired to think about anything else or talk about it.

And then she was back in the world of dreams and nightmares.

CHAPTER 4

*I*n the middle of the night, Ted heard a cougar cry out and he leapt out of bed, ready to grab his rifle, when he realized he was in the clinic, not at the bunkhouse, and the cat that had cried out was a white cougar, tangled in her sheets. And he had no rifle by his side.

Nurse Elsie rushed in.

"She was having a nightmare, I think," Ted said, running his hand over his stubbly face.

"She seems to be sleeping now."

"Yeah, but she about gave me a heart attack."

Elsie smiled at him. "How are you doing?" She was checking Stella's vital signs.

"I'm fine. The headache's gone."

Elsie looked at his chart. "You had a headache? It's not on your chart."

"Yeah, but it's gone." Why didn't Ted remember he hadn't mentioned the headache before, and he shouldn't have now?

"Okay, well, if you need anything, just ring. And if Stella is in pain or really restless, let me know."

"Sure, I will."

Then Elsie left, and Ted climbed back into bed, his heart still pounding furiously. He watched the pretty cougar sleeping soundly and he was glad she wanted to see him further. He just wished she would stay at the Haverton's ranch to recuperate longer, just in case she had issues with the gunshot wounds or the rattlesnake bite.

He heard rain on the rooftop and hitting the window. He loved hearing the sound of rain, normally, but he was even gladder for it tonight since the rain would wash away the blood evidence where Stella had left a trail behind from where she'd been shot all the way to the barn. Otherwise, they were going to have to go and wash it away by hand, wherever they could spot or smell the blood.

Then he finally managed to fall asleep again and the next thing he heard was someone delivering breakfast. That was what he hated about clinics. A body that needed rest couldn't get it. Though he would have been up by now if he'd been at home on the ranch, eating breakfast at the bunkhouse and getting chores done. He guessed the minor concussion he'd had, was worse than he thought.

Stella smiled at him. He was getting used to her being awake when he was asleep. "Elsie said that I nearly gave you a heart attack."

He laughed. "Yeah. You let out a blood curdling cougar cry. Elsie had double-timed it to get here too."

"Sorry about that. I had a nightmare about hunters shooting at me."

"I don't blame you. I would feel the same way. I'm just lucky that when I've ever run into hunters, I've been able to leap up into the rocks and get away from them, or run so fast, they never had a chance. But something like that would definitely give me nightmares. I mean, just being hunted, not even having been shot."

"Here? You've had trouble here before?"

He didn't want her to think it wasn't safe here to run, but they'd had some cases of hunters trespassing on the ranch property before. "A couple of times. We respond to it quickly and with hunter licenses being revoked, heavy fines given, and some jail time, like in this case, it helps to keep people from doing it further. We spread the word, we share it in our local newspaper, all with the hope that hunters will learn not to come here and violate our laws. But there are always those who don't get the word. In your case, killing a white cougar was just too tempting."

"I try not to stay in any one area to run, just in case anyone spies me and captures me on a camera, and everyone descends on the area. But I do need to run as a cougar sometimes. It's just in our blood."

"I agree."

"I was so afraid you would think I was a cougar after the horses. But I guess the horses are used to cougars, and they aren't upset when you shift."

"No. We'll have to scold the dogs, Koda and Zula, though. They should have alerted us way before the hunters began shooting up the place."

She smiled. "They missed seeing me too."

Nurse Mandy Jones came in to take their vital signs then, and said, "Dr. Rugel is coming in to see you and discharge you, Ted. Stella, Dr. Hill is most likely going to keep you for another couple of days."

"No, I need to get back to work."

"They'll understand once you tell them you were shot by hunters. You can't leave the clinic until one of the doctors okays you going home. You don't have anyone to look after you, do you?" Mandy asked.

"No."

"It's for your own good then. If you were to return to work too soon and ended up having to return here, you might have a longer stay."

Stella let out her breath in exasperation. "All right."

Then Mandy left, and Ted pulled the curtain closed and began to get dressed. "I'll sneak food into you," he promised Stella.

She was quiet.

He finished dressing and opened the curtain to see Kate standing there with her arms folded across her chest, waiting for him to open the curtain. He smiled. Caught again!

"She needs to eat what I prescribe for her first."

Stella was smiling at him though.

"I'm free to go, right?" Ted wanted to hang around to be with Stella, to keep her company, but he had chores to do that Hal was counting on him to take care of.

Dr. Rugel entered the room. "Yeah, but with restrictions." He handed Ted the paperwork.

Ted read over the restrictions. "Hell, I can't even lift the kids to give them a horseback ride."

"Right. And if you feel nauseous, dizzy, or have severe headaches, you tell someone at the ranch right away. No heroics."

Ted might as well sit here and visit with Stella. "I'll see you later," Ted said to Stella. "Seems I've got to do light work around the ranch for a few days. I guess I can feed the chickens."

Kate and William smiled at him.

"Kolby's supposed to shadow you and make sure you don't do what you're not supposed to do. He's supposed to do it instead, and believe me, he's eager to prove he can do everything you do and more while you're on restricted duties," Kate said.

"I bet."

"Thanks again, Ted, for coming to my aid," Stella said to Ted.

"I'm glad I was there to come to your aid." He was glad it hadn't come to bloodshed, but if those men had persisted on going after the cougar in their barn—when he was afraid it had been one of their own kind, figuring a real cougar would have run away from the ranch when in danger and not toward it and seeking protection there—he would have opened fire on them.

Wounding them would have been preferable, of course, but if they had retaliated, it would have been a different story.

He squeezed her hand. "I'll come and see you when I'm not doing my light work around the ranch. Tonight."

"Okay, that sounds good. Thanks, Ted."

Then he left, wishing she could stay at the ranch, but they would have to have someone watch over her, and that someone should be the medical staff for now.

But he intended to pick up some white roses for her before he dropped by to see her tonight.

He planned to just drive home, but Kolby came to pick him up, and he realized he had needed a ride since Bill and Ted had come in together and Bill would have driven the pickup home. Ted was going to drive now, but Kolby wouldn't even let him do that. To an extent, Ted was amused.

"Okay, should I sit in the back seat and you can be my chauffeur?" Ted raised his brows.

Kolby laughed. "You always drive, so this time, I get to, and then it'll be back to the old way of doing things. She's hot, isn't she?"

"She's amazing." But seeing all the red blood on her white fur coat had been shocking.

"Bill's not going to try and date her and take her away from us, is he?" Kolby sounded worried.

"No." At least Ted didn't think so, though he had gotten her flowers. "And she's not with us anyway."

"You're going to change that, aren't you? If you don't, I will."

Ted chuckled. "You're too young for her."

"She's a cougar!"

Ted laughed. "I'm going to visit her after work."

"Can I come too?"

"No."

"See? You're afraid I'll win her over."

"No, I'm not."

"Well, Hal might still say someone has to drive you."

Ted groaned.

"Is your head hurting?"

"No."

"Someone has to keep her here."

Ted smiled. "I'm hoping we'll all make her feel welcome, but you know it's up to her whether she wants to be with a family of cougars or not. If she's happy where she's at, and she doesn't want to be with other cougars, except maybe on occasion, then that's the way it will have to be."

"Nah, someone needs to convince her what she's missing out on in life if she doesn't join us," Kolby said.

Ted didn't think of himself as naturally laid back, but about pushing a cougar, any cougar, into wanting to be something they wouldn't be comfortable with? That wasn't him. Long term, he figured it wouldn't work out for the cougar.

"Take me to the jail, will you?" Ted said, wanting to have another good look at the men who had shot Stella.

"Yeah, sure."

When they got there, he and Kolby went inside.

"No way in hell, man," Sims said as Dan charged him with attempted murder.

"We were shooting at the cougar," Braxton said.

"Yeah, no damn person. And if there had been a person there, they would have been killed by the bloody cougar," Clayton said.

"I guess you didn't consider that anyone would have even been in the building when you started shooting at it. We have the rounds that the doctor took out of the victim's wounds, so think again," Dan said.

Ted was glad Dan was throwing the book at them. Kolby just smiled.

* * *

WHEN THEY ARRIVED at the ranch, Tracey came out and gave Ted a hug. "We're so glad you're going to be all right, and Bill tells us Stella is doing fine. He said he would hang around if you needed him to do the ranching chores. He would change his flight plans and leave later, if you want."

"Hell, I forgot all about him leaving tomorrow." Ted enjoyed seeing his brother, though he was glad Bill wouldn't be seeing any more of Stella then. Ted was supposed to drive Bill to the airport.

"Kolby is going to do the driving to the airport, if you feel fine with Bill going home. It's totally up to you. You know we always enjoy it when your brother comes and spends time with us," Tracey said.

Ted looked at Kolby.

Kolby smiled. "I guess you'll need my chauffeur services again."

Then Ted saw Bill headed out of the stables. He smiled and waved. "How are you doing? I was going to come and get you, but Kolby said you never let him drive and he wanted to do it."

Ted shook his head. "I'm doing fine. There's no need for you to hang around unless you want to visit with me longer."

"Nah. You're going to be busy seeing Stella until she leaves, right?"

Ted nodded. "Yep. I promised her I would see her tonight even."

"See? I'll leave first thing in the morning like I planned then. You're sure you're all right?" Bill asked, sounding truly concerned now.

"Yeah, they put me on limited duties, but I didn't need to be."

Bill smiled and slapped him on the shoulder. "Let's get breakfast. Tracey was holding it up for you, though she fed the kids already."

* * *

STELLA RECEIVED ten more vases of flowers from various families around Yuma Town. Now she felt special. If she'd been at the clinic back home, her co-workers would have gotten her a vase of flowers, but nothing like this. It smelled like a bit of floral heaven in the room, like she was in the royal gardens. Even the nurses Elsie, Mandy, who appeared to be about six months pregnant, and Helen Kretchen came in and breathed in the scents and smiled, then went about their business as if they were taking a break from their duties to walk through the gardens.

"Is it always like this, or is it because I'm so rare?" Stella asked Mandy.

"It's always like this when we have an unattached female cougar injured and we are taking care of her," Mandy said. "Now, if it's a male we don't know anything about, probably not."

"Well, it has been wonderful."

Dr. Kate came into the room and said, "In case no one has told you, we have the annual Halloween party coming up. Costumes are not mandatory, but everyone wears them. If you don't have plans, come down and stay with someone, everyone will offer, and you can enjoy the festivities."

That's when Stella noticed some of the pumpkins and fall leaves decorating the room. She enjoyed fall, but she normally didn't do anything for Halloween except give trick-or-treaters candy when they came to her apartment complex. That might be a total of ten kids. She lived in one of those swinging singles complexes. Not that she was swinging, or anything, mainly because she was a shifter, but she liked living in a complex where they didn't have a ton of kids out playing in the parking lot or in the complex itself. The downside of it being a singles place was that there were often wild parties going on, none of which she had been interested in.

"I'll see how things go." Stella didn't want to commit to going and then back out, especially when everyone was being so nice to her.

"Well, we have a western theme going on this year. Some said it wasn't Halloween enough because several members of our community wear western clothes to work in, but we had a vote and that's what was decided."

Now, Stella loved western clothes. And guys dressed in western gear and cowboys.

"Just modern-day clothes, right?"

"Some of us ladies are dressing in hoop skirts. Really, anything goes."

Now that sounded like fun! "Okay, I would like that."

Kate pulled out her phone and showed her the gown she was going to wear. "It's a great site for costumes, and reasonable too. I just don't have any time, or the inclination, to make anything right now." She offered Stella her phone to look at all the gowns.

Stella looked through them. "Is everyone buying from the same company?" She could imagine everyone wearing the same thing.

"Some are, some aren't. I can send you the list of what every-one's wearing if you're worried about buying one that is the same as anyone else has."

Stella gave Kate her email address and figured if she bought a gown, she was going to her first ever Halloween party. Though if something came up, she might not be able to.

* * *

THAT NIGHT, Ted dropped by with a dozen white roses for Stella. She smiled at the thought behind his selection.

"How are you feeling?" Ted pulled over a chair next to the bed and sat down.

"Better. I really think I can go to work on Monday, but I'll need to wear a sling."

"You might not be able to do a lot until you're out of the sling either. Are you sure you don't want to stay at the ranch? You could sleep in one of the rooms of the bunkhouse or you could stay with Tracey and Hal and the kids in the main house. They're ready for either. We have our own kitchen in the bunkhouse, our own living room and even a rec room. So it's not just a place to sleep in."

"I think I'll go home, but thanks for the offer."

"All right. On my way in, Kate told me she invited you to the Halloween party and you could stay with one of the families to attend. Are you going to come?"

"Yeah, I guess so. It sounds like fun. Whose idea was it to wear western clothes?"

"Kolby and mine. We have different cougars who make recommendations each year. If it had been Ricky and Mandy, his mate, we would have a steampunk theme always. One year, we did the Pirates of the Caribbean. So this year, it's a western theme. I'd love to take you, if you would like."

"Sure. I couldn't decide, but Kate showed me some gowns that she and the other ladies have bought, and I went ahead and ordered mine."

"All right. We have it at the ranch this year. So if you stay with us, you won't be needing to go anywhere. Then we'll have pony rides for the kids, hayrides, a corn maze, dancing, and food. We'll turn one of the outer buildings into a haunted house. It will be fun."

She smiled. "That would be. I've never been to a Halloween party, but that sounds like fun."

"We'll run as cougars afterwards before the little ones are too worn out."

That decided it! She was going.

Elsie brought in her dinner, but instead of it being a platter of clinic food, it was a dinner of steak and mashed potatoes and broccoli. "Ted convinced Dr. Kate you needed this to help you heal faster and that it works well for him. Doc said that you should be fine eating this."

Stella couldn't believe Ted had gone through the trouble to convince the doctor to let her eat what she wanted to. Now she realized why Kate had asked her what she loved best to eat this morning after breakfast—in just a chatty kind of way.

"Courtesy of Ted," Elsie added, smiling at him, then leaving them alone. Then she returned with another tray. "He said you might not want to eat in front of him, so he made a dinner for himself to enjoy while he keeps you company." She set it on the other table, and he pulled it over to the chair so he could eat next to Stella.

"Now this takes the cake. A first date with a cougar in a clinic bed—with a four-star meal." She took a bite of her steak. "This is perfect."

"I grilled the steaks at Kate and Leyton's place just a few minutes ago and made the mashed potatoes and broccoli. I thought you might need some good home-cooked food and their house is right behind the clinic."

"Oh, this is just great. The other is fine, but it's more institutionalized. Okay, I'll take you up on your offer for me to stay at the bunkhouse for another day or two, if Kate says I can leave the clinic soon."

"Yes," he said with a fist pump.

She laughed, but she continued to enjoy her steak then too. "It's just delicious."

"I would sneak you out to see a movie at the ranch with me because Kate won't give you a pass, but—"

"We can watch a movie together here. All we need is popcorn."

He laughed. "I'll be right back."

He couldn't be asking Kate if they could have popcorn. They would be full by the time they ate their meals.

When Ted returned, he was smiling.

"You did not ask Kate if we could have popcorn, did you?" Stella couldn't help but be amused.

"Yeah, she said they have some in the lounge. I'll make it for us as soon as we want some."

She smiled. "We're going to be full."

But after they ate, they talked about all kinds of stuff, and by the time he cleared away their plates and they settled in to watch a movie, she was ready for some popcorn.

"I'll go get it." He left the room and ran into Mandy.

"The furthermost righthand cabinet over the microwave," Mandy said.

"Thanks."

Any guy who would do this much for Stella while she was in the clinic, and even before that, and was a cougar, was worth spending more time with, she decided.

Then they settled on a western movie and shared popcorn. She was glad her right shoulder hadn't been injured since she did so much with her right arm.

Now she was ready to leave the clinic, have more delicious meals, and sleep without interruption any time she needed to.

When the movie ended, Ted leaned over and kissed her forehead. "I'll return tomorrow night to have dinner with you and hopefully, you'll be able to leave the next day."

"It's a deal."

CHAPTER 5

*W*hen Ted left, Stella was feeling so much better physically. Elsie came in and said, "Kate said if you have Tracey and the others to watch out for you, you can leave here tomorrow afternoon. We'll let them know you'll need transportation out there. They can take you to your Jeep in the impound lot or take it to the ranch for when you're ready to leave and return home."

"Okay, thanks. That sounds good." She was thrilled. She hoped she could sit out on the porch and watch the cowboys at work firsthand.

Then she tried to sleep, but the nightmare returned.

She just had to reach the barn, just several hundred yards across the field where the grass was short. She could do it. Sprint at forty-five miles per hour. Leap into the barn. Hope that no one at the horse ranch saw her run in there before she could shift. Then the men saw her out in the open and closed the distance, not calling out, not alerting the ranch hands if there were any about. The hunters were going to catch her. They were going to shoot her full of holes. They were nearly there. And they fired at her. One bullet after another, the rounds pinging off the metal building and she was afraid she was going to get hit by some of the ricocheting bullets. But she didn't feel that she'd taken any more hits.

That would soon change if they came into the barn and found her bleeding as a cougar in there and finished her off. She leapt up into the hayloft and moved around a bundle of hay and tried to shift. She heard men shouting at the hunters to drop their weapons. But they wouldn't comply. It was like an old-western shootout. The men would be eyeballing each other, but no one would concede.

Then she heard a man coming into the barn. One of the ranch hands? She couldn't shift. Damn, she couldn't even lift her head. She heard him close the doors to the barn. And then he said he was a cougar, and he would like her to stay with him. And he would take her to the Halloween party. But it would be here. Right here. At the horse ranch with other cougars like her. But not like her. She was a rare white cougar, and they would gawk at her, but no. She would be wearing a beautiful blue gown, her shoulders exposed, and she would look like a western princess, her knight in shining armor in western boots, chaps, and a Stetson, coming to her rescue on a white stallion.

She startled awake and smelled eggs and bacon and hash brown potatoes and saw Ted bringing her another home-cooked meal.

"Fresh eggs, even," he said. "Store bought bacon though."

"I...I thought you were coming for dinner, then they said I could join you all on your ranch this afternoon, so I thought—"

"I'll pick you up this afternoon. I just wanted to make sure you had a good hearty breakfast to get you through until then."

She smiled. "Wow. Just, wow. Thanks, Ted. This is great. I've never had fresh eggs before. They're great."

He looked at all the flowers.

"Either everyone who wanted to has already given me flowers, or you've chased them all off with bringing me meals and your own roses."

He chuckled. "I had to do something to make you feel as

though we hope your next visit to Yuma Town will be more peaceful and fun, and less painful and stressful."

"You've done a great job with that. And so has everyone else. Even the clinic staff has been wonderful. This is so much different than if I'd had to go to a human medical facility."

"It is. I'll take you home before we have lunch. Tracey's making something for everyone. We often do our own thing because she's busy with the kids, though when they get bigger, she vows to start doing some more of her work with the U.S. Fish and Wildlife Services."

"I heard her call out to the hunters that she was a special agent. I felt bad that I had brought trouble to the ranch. I hadn't thought that there might be women and children there, not to mention the danger to livestock because the hunters had come after me."

"I don't think any of us would have believed they would do that. We were just glad we could stop them and come to your aid. Even though you weren't with the family, we still consider you family."

She hadn't felt like she'd belonged anywhere for a long time. It felt good.

Then Ted had to leave, but he kissed her on the forehead before he left, and she grabbed his hand and made him kiss her mouth too. After all he had done for her? She wanted to.

Elsie came in and Ted finally ended the kiss, but not until *after* the nurse got an eyeful. He was definitely an alpha male.

"I'll see you in a little while. When is Kate releasing her?" he asked.

"She can go at eleven," Dr. Rugel said, coming into the room. He looked at the clock on the wall. "In four hours."

"Good. We'll be in time for lunch at the house then." Ted said goodbye to everyone, then took off, texting on his phone as he went.

* * *

TED HURRIED to decorate the bunkhouse before he had to pick up Stella to take her out to the ranch. He just hadn't had the time, or the inclination, but with being so restricted on duties, he figured he would get it done, now that Stella was here staying with him, and not just Kolby. He hated to admit he wanted to decorate for her—to make everything perfect.

He draped fall leaf garlands across the fireplace mantle and hung a fall leaf wreath on the front door. He set out a big white pumpkin with a lantern and autumn foliage surrounding it in the center of the dining room table.

He pulled out a couple of scarecrows to set out on the front porch and saw Tracey was out helping the kids paint faces on their pumpkins. Ted went over to see what she needed him to do.

She smiled brightly. "You can help the kids with their painting."

Ted frowned. That wasn't what he had in mind.

"Hal's helping Kolby with the horses. You can help me with the Halloween decorations. A bunch of our friends, Chase and Shannon, Travis and Bridget, Jack and Dottie, they'll all be over later to help do some more decorations for Halloween. You can help with that later."

"Okay." He sat down on the ground with the kids, who were already covered in paint, and helped them to paint faces on their pumpkins.

"I want a smiley face," Denise said.

"Mine is sticking his tongue out," Liam said.

Ted glanced at Tracey. She just smiled as she painted her own jack-o'-lantern.

"No, not like that," Denise said as he painted a smile on her pumpkin. "She has a pink mouth, not red."

Smiling, Ted shook his head.

"Red and white paint mixed will give you pink," Tracey said.

"I think this goes beyond my duties as foreman."

Tracey laughed as Evan Chase sat on his lap, making it even more difficult to mix paint and apply a mouth to Denise's pumpkin.

"Blue eyes," Denise said.

He made two blue eyes.

"A pink nose."

He added that. Then Tabitha handed her paintbrush to Ted and said, "Mine too."

Of course Hal and Kolby had to smile as they saw him sitting there painting a pumpkin and getting paint on himself too. Or maybe it was paint from Denise's brush.

* * *

STELLA WAS SO grateful to the staff who took care of her at the clinic and she left her flowers there so they could give them to anyone who would like them. When Ted arrived, he took her in a wheelchair to a black pickup truck. She hadn't expected that. She could walk, for heaven's sake, but when she tried to stand, she did feel a little woozy. He swept her up in his arms and put her in the truck.

She frowned at him and smiled. "You have pink polka dots."

"What?" He looked down at his hands and chuckled. "Hal is not letting me do a lot of work still and Tracey put me in charge of helping the kids paint pumpkins. I guess I missed some spots when I washed up."

"That's funny. About my Jeep…," she said.

"We can take it to the ranch, if you would like, or leave it where it is."

"I don't want to put anyone out, but I would like it at the ranch so when I'm ready to go I can just leave."

"Sure. I'll make sure we get it. No problem at all."

She looked over the town as they headed out to the ranch and she thought how cute and well-maintained everything was: the sheriff's department, a park in the center of the town, a bakery, a boutique and everything was decorated for Halloween. When they finally reached the ranch, she realized just how big the place was with the main ranch house, a couple of barns, other outbuildings, and the bunkhouse, several horses, cattle, corrals, and a couple of dogs running around playing with each other.

"Where are the kids?" She had been looking forward to seeing them.

"I imagine the kids are taking their naps about now."

"Oh, okay." Then she saw the cute pumpkins. "Did you paint all those?"

"Unfortunately, yes. Have me paint a barn and I can do a great job. Fences? Same thing. Pumpkin painting? I'm totally out of my element."

She laughed. "Well, I think you did an outstanding job and when you have kids someday, you'll have the technique down pat."

"Hopefully, I won't have that many all at once."

She smiled. "For your mate's sake, I would have to agree."

She was going to get the door herself, but it was harder to do while wearing a sling. Suddenly he was there, opening her door, and lifting her out of the truck, then setting her on the ground. Her hero.

While she'd been at the clinic wearing a clinic gown, the ladies had washed her clothes that had been in her car, but she realized she didn't have a change of clothes for tomorrow. No toiletries either.

Ted took her inside the bunkhouse, and she was amazed to see how lovely it was. She'd halfway expected it to have used furniture, thrown in there for a bunch of raucous cowboys to sit on, but instead she found beautiful leather couches and chairs, paneled walls and bookshelves, a fireplace, large screen TV, a lovely kitchen with granite counters, stainless steel fridge, double sinks, island counter, a place that would be great for baking cookies or having a pizza party. Her apartment had a pint-sized kitchen so she was really wowed to see this one.

The dining room was just as lovely with eight chairs seated at the long rectangular table. Horse statues and paintings added to the cheery bunkhouse.

He showed her the guest bedroom first. "Kolby's room is down the hall and mine is the last one. I have the master bedroom suite. The bathroom is there, and Tracey picked up some things for you to use while you are here. Shampoo, toothbrush, toothpaste, body wash. And she bought you some clothes to wear also, judging on the size of the clothes they found in your Jeep."

"Oh, how sweet of her. How did they get into my Jeep? They didn't break the lock, did they?"

"No. Dr. Kate asked you when you were coming out of anesthesia what the combination was. We were able to get in after that."

"Oh, I don't remember that. All you need to do is drug me and I'll give you anything, I guess."

He smiled. "Tracey said we can join them at the house for lunch, or if you think you would be more comfortable here where it's quieter, than she said we could do that. It's up to you."

"After all she's done for me, I want to thank her for it. Let's go over to the house. Unless you're worried Tracey might make you paint more pumpkins."

He chuckled. "Yeah, no telling." He walked Stella to the main house but kept an eye on her to make sure she didn't get faint like she did when she was getting out of the wheelchair before she climbed into his truck.

"Your bunkhouse doesn't look anything like what I expected."

"Old worn-out furniture? Yeah, we had that."

She raised a brow at him.

"When Hal mated Tracey, she redid the main house and then

came out to the bunkhouse to begin 'fixing' it up. We didn't know what to expect. And at first, we had to stay at the main house for a while. She had everything renovated, including a master bedroom and bathroom for the foreman, and redid all of the kitchen and the bathrooms. All new furniture throughout. We didn't know what we were missing out on until she redid everything. From the horse paintings to the statues, re-paneling the walls and floors, granite countertops, all new appliances in the kitchen. It made it a real home for us and a place we are proud of. The housekeeper keeps after the main house and the bunkhouse too, but we try to tidy up after ourselves also. Something my mother ingrained in us. My sister, Josephine, and brother— triplets—and I had to clean and cook and wash. Not just my mom and sister. It was a good lesson for us. I love to cook. Not just grill out of doors when the weather is nice. So it was great having a new kitchen."

"That's wonderful. You should see my tiny apartment and kitchen."

When they reached the house, Tracey ushered them in. "We're all ready for lunch."

"Thanks so much for everything," Stella said. "You've all been so kind."

"Will you shift for us?" one of her girls asked.

"Yeah, Mommy said if we were extra good and you wanted to —" Then the boy's jaw dropped as he looked at Stella's arm in a sling. "Oh, she said if you were still hurt, you couldn't."

"I will be back for the Halloween party," she said. "I'll be fine by then. Though if I'm better tomorrow, I could remove the sling and test out shifting. No running as a cougar, but just to show you my white coat."

"That's if she can," Hal said, coming down the hall from the bathroom, looking like he had just washed up for lunch.

Kolby came in the front door. "Sorry, I'm late."

"Where's Bill?" Stella asked.

"I took him to the airport this morning before I had breakfast with you at the clinic. He meant to say goodbye, but he didn't want to mess up anything between us," Ted said.

She frowned at him.

"Hey, I didn't tell him anything was going on between us. He just assumed it. Anyway, he's a great brother." Ted smiled at her.

She sighed. "I hope everyone's not going to too much trouble over me."

"No, we're always glad to meet other cougars like us," Tracey said, as everyone helped set out the food.

CHAPTER 6

*L*ater that afternoon, Stella had to take a nap. She wished she hadn't had to, because she wanted to see Ted and the others doing their cowboy work. But she could see why the doctors had wanted to keep her at the clinic another day. She needed the rest and she wanted to be recuperated enough to go to work on Tuesday.

"You call us," Ted said, giving her his phone number and the Havertons'. Not Kolby's, she noticed. "When you feel up to it, you can come out and watch us."

She smiled. "Thanks, I'd like that." She hadn't been expecting Koda and Zula, the Australian shepherds, to join her in the guest room. She thought they should have been out with the guys, working cattle or something. But they must have entered through the cougar door and had come to see her.

She smiled at them. "What are the two of you doing in here? Hiding from work?" She thought of making them go outside and then she would lock the cougar door, if she had to, but they curled up next to her bed and they were so cute, she couldn't make them. She loved animals, loved dogs and cats, though her adoptive parents wouldn't let her have any growing up. And she couldn't have them at her apartment—no pets allowed. But whenever she would go to a park, she had to admire pet owners' dogs, talk to them, and pet them, if she could.

She hoped the dogs wouldn't get into trouble. She figured Ted wouldn't be too upset with her if he learned where they were. And she hadn't made them leave the bunkhouse.

It wasn't long after she laid down that she was sound asleep and dreaming about a beautiful day—though she thought she heard Ted chuckle softly under his breath, the dogs stir, but then he said, "Stay," and left the guest room. She thought that had happened, unless she was just dreaming it. She couldn't open her eyes and look for anything, she was so tired, and then her worst nightmare returned—hunters with her in their sights as she ran as a white cougar, up on top of the cliffs, down the other side, and racing through the tall meadow grasses for her life.

TED WAS glad Stella had decided to stay with them for a couple of days, but after lunch, she appeared so worn out, it had worried him. Maybe they'd pushed her a little too much. He didn't want to have to return her to the clinic, but he would, if he thought she needed further medical care.

He couldn't believe Koda and Zula had sneaked off to be with her. Well, sneak wasn't exactly the word he should use to describe their behavior. When Ted was sick and in bed during the day, they would curl up next to his bed, so it appeared they'd taken her in as one of their pack too. Which he thought was cute. The funniest thing was when he went looking for them, and Kolby had pointed to the bunkhouse, Ted had expected to see Stella awake and petting them, and not sleeping while they slept beside her bed. He wondered if she had known they were in there. They both raised their heads to acknowledge him, waiting for a command, and he whispered the command, "Stay," and motioned with his hand to emphasize he meant it. Then he left the guest room and went outside where Kolby was mounted and waiting for him to help with the cattle.

"What were Koda and Zula doing?" Kolby asked.

Ted smiled. "Sleeping next to the bed where Stella was sound asleep."

Kolby glanced back at the bunkhouse as Ted mounted his horse. "And you didn't make them come with you?"

"Nah, they have a job. They're protecting Stella. You know how it is if either of us get sick or injured. They stay with whoever is bedridden."

Kolby smiled. "You're a pushover when it comes to Stella."

"Isn't it true that they come to sympathize with us when we're sick?" Ted asked as they rode off together.

"Yeah, I hate to admit it, but you're right."

* * *

LATER, Ted was raking up the yard to make a pile of yellow, orange, and red leaves for the kids to play in. Sometimes work was just for fun. The kids all had their miniature rakes out. The rakes were adult quality with wooden handles and metal teeth, but kid-sized and the kids loved them. There was no time like the present to teach kids how to clean up things, but of course, they were going to play in the pile of leaves afterward, so that kind of ruined the notion of "cleaning up" the yard.

The dogs had left the house to potty and were snapping at the leaves, every time Ted tossed a big pile of them on the mountain he was building.

Still, it was one of his favorite fall adventures he played with the kids since they were preschoolers. He might be all business when he was teaching new ranch hands the ropes, but when he had a moment to play with the kids, he was doing it. And Tracey appreciated it. He noticed that not only was Kolby watching him, but the new hands were too. The one was a sixteen-year-old car thief, Jasper Holliday, that the CSF agent, Chet Kensington, brought to Yuma Town to face the consequences of his reckless behavior for stealing cars, and subsequently he was now working at the ranch as a hand, closely supervised by everyone.

Ted raised his brows at the new ranch hands as if to say—don't you have a job to do? But they were getting too big a kick out of seeing this other side of him. Just as he fell into the leaves and the kids pounced on him—instead of picking their own part of the leave pile to dive in, he saw Stella watching him and smiling. The dogs were barking and in on the muddle with them right away.

He chuckled. Caught in the act. He got out of the leaves and brushed them off his clothes, then headed over to see Stella, handing the rake to Kolby on the way there. "Teach the other ranch hands how to rake, will you?"

Kolby laughed. "I didn't ever think you'd let me play in the leaves with the kids."

Ted smiled and joined Stella on the porch.

"Hey, you guys, believe me, this is a new side of Ted you rarely see. Enjoy it while you can," Kolby told the new ranch hands.

"How are you feeling?" Ted asked Stella, taking hold of her hand.

"I'm feeling much better, thank you."

Earlier, he had been breaking a horse, which he figured she would have been more interested in seeing since she seemed fascinated with anything cowboy related. He would like to show off his ranching skills. Giving the four-year-old Haverton children pony rides or raking leaves wasn't exactly the kind of work real cowboys usually did.

Kolby was raking the leaves onto the pile and the other ranch hands were using the small rakes to help him. Tracey finally came outside to have the kids take their naps, and the guys were left to fill giant pumpkin bags full of leaves. At the end of Halloween, they would run the leaves through the mulcher and have mulch for Tracey's gardens in the spring.

Stella smiled. "That was so cute. I saw you giving the kids horseback rides. They sure learn to ride young."

"Yeah, I was the same age when I learned how to ride. I never thought anything of it. It was like riding a bike." He smiled at her, glad she didn't think it was too silly of him. He enjoyed playing with the kids. And he was making them future riders, maybe even cowboys and cowgirls. Though they might go into their mom or dad's line of work—working at the U.S. Fish Wildlife Service or with the sheriff's department. Then he noticed Stella was not wearing the sling any longer.

"How is your arm? And your leg?" he asked.

"Oh, so much better. I needed to get some sleep. Now I feel so much better."

"Good. How do you feel about us going for a ride? Have you ever ridden?"

"Yes, just on a trail horse on one of those hour-long trips."

"Then I'm going to have to make a cowgirl out of you."

She smiled.

"If you think you can ride. I'll help you up on the horse and then we can take a short trip. I don't want you to overdo it, but if you want to, I'd love to take you out for a little ride."

"I'd love it."

"Okay." He got a couple of horses saddled for them and helped Stella onto the smaller of the two. "Mine is a blue dun appaloosa named Pablo. And the chestnut appaloosa you're riding is Celestina. They're great for beginners and very gentle."

Koda and Zula were prancing around outside the stables and he knew they wanted to run with them.

"Do you mind taking the dogs with us? It's good exercise for them. I don't always take them, but they're always eager to go with me when I just take a ride for the pleasure of it."

"Yes, sure. I love the dogs. They're so energetic and fun to be with."

Then he mounted his horse, and he took her for a ride. He was done with his chores for the moment. It was time to play with the she-cat. Besides, this was one of the joys of working on a ranch. Riding.

"Come, Koda, Zula!" And the two dogs raced off to join them, running circles around each other, chasing off into the distance and then returning faithfully to their master.

They would be dead tired when they returned home like they always were when he took them on horseback rides.

"It's beautiful out here. I love it. I think it's safer riding a horse though, then running as a cougar," she said.

"It's normally very safe. I'll take you to the waterfalls, but if you get too tired, we'll turn back." He was glad Stella had been sleeping all this time, but he worried that maybe she should have stayed at the clinic if she was still so worn out from her wounds.

"I can make it. I had seen it on a map of the area and had planned to see it before I was shot."

"I'm still pissed off at the men who shot you." Then he let out his breath and changed topics. "If you had made it to the falls, you would have smelled all the cougars that have been in the area."

"And wondered what was up," she said. "I doubt I would have connected them with the idea they were all shifters. How did you come to work here?" she asked.

"When I left home, I ended up at a human-run horse ranch and I worked there until Hal came to buy some horses from him to start his own ranch. Once I realized he was a cougar, I was eager to work for him as a ranch hand. I made sure Hal bought the best horses and got a fair price from my boss, Bob Johnson. I really appreciated Bob for giving me a job in the beginning after I left home. I knew my business when it came to taking care of horses on my dad's quarter horse ranch, Whispering Oaks Ranch. So I was a good hire for Bob, though he said I was a little rough around the edges—getting into fights with some of the other ranch hands—mostly due to my youth and being a cougar, and being from Texas—as if we didn't know how to run a ranch there—instead of being from Colorado. I knew so much about the business and was always telling the other ranch hands how to do their jobs better. I didn't win a lot of points."

She laughed.

"Hal has eight-hundred prime acres of land. It's a cougar—and horses'—paradise. The cougars have parties here often. Great for weddings and all kinds of celebrations."

"That's a lot of acreage."

"Yeah, it's great for running as cougars. Everyone comes out here when they want to."

"And no hunters."

He smiled. "Not usually, right. But rattlesnakes, that's another story. We have to be on the lookout for them in the summer especially. Usually we can avoid them, but you were wounded and trying to keep out of the hunters' reach, so it's understandable that you were bitten. Normally, you would have been able to run so fast, dodge so quickly, you would have been fine."

"Yeah, I've never been bitten by a snake of any kind any time I've been out running as a cougar, so I'm sure that had all to do with it."

* * *

STELLA WAS SO excited to be actually riding a horse beside Ted, and not on a trail horse that tried to knock her off at any chance he had. She loved seeing the mountains in the distance, the river, forest, acres of pastureland and off in the distance, she could see Rainbow Falls. "This is just beautiful."

"It is. I'll have to bring you here sometime when the sun is setting."

That was the great thing about being cougars and being able to see at night, though they would do better running as cougars then.

"As cougars?" she asked.

"Yeah, but once you're fully healed. Feeling better while resting is one thing, running and working the muscles that were injured is another."

"Right." She knew she would be sore after riding the horse too, since she hadn't ridden one in years. She remembered being sore that time.

They were drawing closer to the waterfalls and she decided if she continued to see Ted, she wanted to always come here. Just the sound of the water cascading down the rocks made her feel good. "Oh, I love this."

"Yeah, we all do. It's one of the favorite spots for romantic excursions and for families to get away and enjoy nature."

She laughed. "I bet the kids like splashing in the water."

"They do. We take turns bringing them here. We actually have Carver Falls also, near Lake Buchanan, where Deputy Sheriff Chase Buchanan and his mate, Shannon, own Pinyon Pines Cabin Resort. It's great for playing in too."

"I'll have to check it out sometime also."

Then they dismounted and he tied the horses to a tree branch.

She felt it was too cold to actually get out and swim or anything, especially with it being fall, the breeze whipping little white caps on the pond. If she hadn't been so recently injured, she would have stripped and shifted into her cougar and swam across to see the waterfall, stand under it, and check out the area behind it. In her fur coat, she would have been fine.

As if he knew what she was thinking, he put his arm around her waist and squeezed. "We can return here when you're all healed up and swim over there as cougars. In the summer, it's really a hot spot for cougars."

"I bet. It would be a lot of fun." Now this was the kind of place she was looking for. Though she wanted to climb the cliffs as a cougar and reach all the way to the top to see the world before her. That was all about being a cougar. Nobody could touch them there.

"And climbing. Once you're healed up. We could climb it as humans, but everyone prefers to climb it as cougars." He released her and picked up a flat stone and skimmed it across the pond. It skipped three times.

She tried it then and actually skipped a rock twice. She had never tried that before. Being around Ted, she was having lots of firsts, she realized.

Before it got too late, he helped her mount Celestina and then he mounted Pablo and they headed back to the bunkhouse.

"What would you like to eat? How about tacos? Enchiladas? Fajitas?" Ted asked.

"Steak fajitas?" Stella loved them. Whenever she ate at a Mexican restaurant, that's what she ordered. None of that hamburger fajita mixture. That was fine in tacos though.

"Yeah, sure, guacamole, shredded lettuce, shredded cheese, sauteed onions, and green and red bell peppers."

"You've got a deal." She smiled. "You're going to make me not want to return home."

"That's the whole idea."

"You're doing a great job of it." She'd never been around a guy who was so into wanting to make her feel welcome, special, that he enjoyed hanging out with her as much as she enjoyed hanging out with him.

The breeze swept across them and she was feeling a little chilly. She was glad they were returning to the bunkhouse. That's all she needed was to end up with a cold on top of everything else. Sure, they got over colds quicker than humans, but they could still get sick for a few days with them. And she certainly didn't want to catch a cold and then give it to Ted after all he'd done for her.

He saw her shiver, so he stopped his horse, and untied a blanket rolled up on the back of his saddle. Then he gave it to her. "I should have realized you might get cold as soon as the sun began to set. Sorry. You aren't really dressed to be running around out here at night."

She pulled the blanket around her shoulders and held on with one hand, holding the reins with the other.

When they returned to the ranch, he helped her dismount, and he showed her the horses in the stable. She enjoyed seeing all the horses that seemed eager to see her too as they poked their noses out to let her pet them, but then Ted said, "I've got some last-minute chores to do and once everything is taken care of, I'll join you at the bunkhouse. Why don't you go inside and get warmed up and rest? Watch some TV and take it easy. I'll start the fajitas as soon as I'm done."

"Do you want me to start them?" She didn't want him to think he had to wait on her hand and foot.

"No, really, I've got it. I want you to rest. I know you don't want to stay long here, and you'll want to head back to work, so you need to be well-rested."

Even so, he went inside and started a nice warm, cheery fire for her, and she loved the hominess of the place and curled up on the couch under a soft blanket.

"Okay, thanks, Ted." She was chilled and tired, and she wouldn't mind just cuddling up in a blanket and watching something—with him.

* * *

LATER THAT NIGHT when Ted was finished with his chores, glad Stella had done what the doctor had ordered—gotten some rest—he went inside the bunkhouse.

"Hey," he said, checking on her first before he showered and fixed dinner. "How do you feel?"

"Tired. I think I overdid it a bit. You were right in making me go inside to rest. Are you sure I can't help you make dinner?"

"No. You just enjoy your movie." He looked in the fridge. "Hmm, on second thought, how about I make us pork ribs, mashed potatoes, and spinach, if that sounds good to you. I don't have any bell peppers or onions. I'll have to grocery shop for the other items and fix the fajitas for you another time."

"Yeah, sure, that would be just perfect."

Once he started the meal, he said, "I'm going to take a quick shower." After his shower, the food was done, and he set it out on the dining room table and she joined him, setting out glasses of iced water for them.

"I'm sorry for the circumstances, but I'm glad you're here."

"I am too. Where is Kolby?" she asked.

"Eating up at the main house."

"So we can be alone?"

"Yeah. If he's dating—uhm, seeing a woman and wants to entertain here, I eat up at the main house, or eat in town. We try to give each other some space."

"That's so nice. It would make it difficult otherwise to have a relationship. Does Kolby have anyone special in his life yet?"

"He has dated. But he hasn't found the right woman yet."

They sat down to eat.

"The meal is delicious," she said. "Thanks, for making it."

"You're so welcome. I want to keep seeing you."

She smiled. "I'd like that."

When they finished the meal, he cleaned the dishes, and they watched a western show, cuddling together and later having popcorn and hot cocoa before it was time to go to bed.

She decided she didn't want to sleep alone. She hadn't when Ted had stayed with her in the same clinic room. Maybe it wasn't the same as sleeping in the same bed, but she wanted that. Wanted to be with a cougar like him. "Can I stay with you?"

He smiled down at her. "Hell, yeah." He grabbed up her clothes and toiletries from the guest room and carried them into his room.

CHAPTER 7

*S*tella hadn't expected to see the beautiful, western-themed bedroom with a heavy, rustic pine bed frame, the legs and headboard trimmed in leather and brass studs. The bedspread was a southwestern design of rusts, light gray, and navy blue, and a large window was featured behind the headboard. Matching pine bedside tables had large brass knobs, and horse paintings graced the walls.

The bedroom was large and had a winged leather chair and a rustic pine desk complete with a computer and a chest at the foot of the bed that might hold blankets for winter. It was really like a presidential suite for a foreman, she thought. "Did Tracey decorate in here too?"

"Yeah. We had the large room, but it was really bland. Now it's country elegant. I feel like a rancher baron."

She chuckled. "You look like one."

"The bathroom's in here," he said, giving her a tour.

A large glassed-in shower, whirlpool tub, double sink, toilet in its own private closet. Just spectacular. "I have about half the size of your bathroom in my apartment. No whirlpool tub. Just the standard tub and shower all in one. No toilet in a private closet. This is the life."

"Yeah, it's pretty nice. Tracey redid all the fixtures in there."

"She appreciates you."

"She appreciates everyone who works for the family. I couldn't have been gladder when she mated the boss man. It showed a side of him we'd never thought we would see. And then he became a family man before we knew it, and I didn't expect to be included in that much of the family happenings once the kids came. The next thing I know, I'm an uncle to the quadruplets."

"That's great, and this is so nice. When you were sleeping, Bill said you have a nephew, Scott, who's in the army. What does he think about the kids?"

"Bill and I are only ten years older than him. His dad was our father's brother and he had him late in life. He has come down here once to see the family and of course they called him Uncle Scott and Aunt Nicole. They adore the kids."

Then Ted helped Stella into the soft flannel pajama top, trying not to hurt her arm, and she was glad Tracey had gotten her a shirt that buttoned instead of pulled over her head. Then Ted helped Stella into a matching pair of pajama bottoms.

Ted put on a pair of hot chili pajama pants, no top, which made him sexy as all get out.

When she climbed into bed, she thought she'd found a bit of heaven. "Hmm, this bed is like sleeping on a cloud."

"Yeah, it is, just the way I like it. Now you tell me if I bother you at all. I don't want to hurt you in the middle of the night."

She moved next to him and snuggled her face against his chest. "I'll try not to growl or bite you, if I hurt in the middle of the night."

He smiled and turned off the lights and kissed the top of her head. "If you need anything at any time, you let me know."

* * *

TED COULDN'T BELIEVE his fortune in meeting the she-cat. He wasn't going to offer that she join him in his room because of her injuries, so he was thrilled when she asked if she could.

He texted Kolby: *You can come home now. Stella's staying with me so try not to disturb her.*

Yeah, well, try not to disturb my sleep.

Ted had no intention of making love to Stella, even though he wanted to. He hoped he wouldn't bump her and hurt her injuries in the middle of the night. But if she wanted to be with him, he wanted to be there for her.

* * *

WHEN STELLA finally woke to hearing Ted and Kolby in the kitchen making breakfast the next morning, she grabbed her phone off the bedside table and groaned, her arm and leg still sore. But she had to call in to work before they worried something bad had happened to her. Like it had, actually.

"Hey, Tori, I'm recuperating after being shot at a ranch near Yuma Town while visiting friends. I'll be coming in on Tuesday," Stella said.

"No, way, Stella," Tori said when she told her the news. "Are you sure you're going to be okay?

"Yeah, I had to have an antivenom for a rattlesnake bite too."

"You're pulling my leg."

It did sound pretty unreal. "No, I wish I was. I had to receive blood for the gunshot wounds. The only thing that saved my life was I was in a barn at the time and the walls slowed down the bullets. Anyway, I'm really sore and tired, but I'll be back at work tomorrow. I'll be home tonight." Though she was thinking she should just come in on Wednesday instead. Yet, she wanted to show them her wounds before they were completely healed, or they might think she had made the whole thing up. But why not just say she had a bad cold or the flu, or something?

"Where can we send flowers to?"

This got tricky. Normally, she probably would have still been in a hospital. But she didn't want to lie about that and get caught up in the lie. "I'm at the Haverton's ranch. There's no need to send flowers or anything. I'll be back at work tomorrow."

"Really, are you sure?"

"Yeah." Which Stella realized it sounded like maybe she really had been making the whole thing up.

"Okay, well, you let us know if you need anything, or want us to drive you home, or, well, take care of you at your apartment or anything."

Stella smiled. "Thanks, I appreciate it." Then they ended the call and she laid back in the bed for a few minutes, not wanting to get out of bed.

Finally, Ted peeked in on her and smiled.

She smiled back. "Okay, I told work I wasn't coming in. What's on the agenda?"

"Rest for you, Halloween decorating and ranching duties for me, but first, a nice big breakfast." He pulled a big robe out of the closet and said, "Why don't you wear this and you can shower or whatever you want after breakfast, just chill out on the couch and rest. We don't want you to do too much."

"Thanks, Ted." She got up then and put on the robe, slipped on the slippers Tracey had gotten her, and thought how much nicer this was than the clinic garb.

Then she had breakfast with Ted and Kolby and after they cleaned up and took off to do ranch work, she took her shower, finally dressed, and headed outdoors to watch Ted taking care of things on the ranch. They were decorating more for Halloween, but as soon as he saw her, he wouldn't let her do anything but sit on the porch of the main house and watch him and the others do all the work. With comfy pillows propping her up on the rocking chair and even a thermos of hot spiced tea that Tracey had brought Stella, she thought this was the best way to recuperate.

Stella was fascinated as he went about his chores and she thought he might even be showing off a little. Which she thought was cute.

They had lunch with the Havertons later, and then she went to sit out on the porch again to watch all the activities. The kids were playing on bales of hay, but then Tracey told Ted to go inside with Stella to make some scarecrows and he saluted Tracey, then escorted Stella inside the house. Both Koda and Zula came in to lie by their feet at the couch. If Ted was through working, they were ready to join him and take a snooze. She had to lean down and pet them.

Then Stella sat back up, ready to get to work.

"Tracey wants you to rest more and get warmed up." Ted started a fire in the fireplace.

Stella had been feeling a bit chilled so she was glad they had gone inside.

"I've got to get started on making some of these scarecrows." Ted brought out a bunch of worn jeans and western shirts, some old pillowcases, a box of safety pins, and some bandanas and carried them into the living room where they were going to watch a movie. "You can sit there and see me create them. Just rest."

"No way. I've never made one before, and I'm helping too." She was eager to assist him with creating scarecrows. This would be fun, and she'd finally get to do something to help with decorating for Halloween like she'd wanted to from the beginning.

"Okay, ready for your first lesson?" He brought out a stack of old newspapers and a sack full of plastic sacks and set them on the coffee table.

"I sure am."

"Great. First, button, zip or close the shirts and pants." He brought out a spool of string and a couple of pairs of scissors.

She could certainly do that. She began buttoning all the shirts.

He was cutting off lengths of string. Then she began fastening all the fasteners on the pants. "How did you learn to do this?"

"Tracey had me help her last year, then she gave me the project this year since I was so good at it. A bunch of us are going to get together to make a lot more of them, but I wanted to get started on some."

"And the two on the front porch? Did you make them?"

"Yeah, Kolby and I made them last year, and we liked them so much, we just stored them for this year." He started crumpling up the newspaper.

"They're really cute. I would have saved them too." She finished fastening all the clothes.

This was fun. But especially because she was doing it with Ted while they were half-watching a thriller on TV, the fire crackling in the fireplace and he paused to wash the ink off his hands, then made them steaming cups of spiced apple cider. Then he was back to crumpling paper. After that, he began to stuff the pillow-cases with the paper.

"Tie strings around the shirt arms and pants legs to close them," he said. "Then we stuff them with the plastic bags or crumpled up newspaper. And then just use the safety pins to attach the shirt to the pants at the waist."

She began stuffing the jeans with plastic bags. "Are all these clothes yours?"

"Nah. Everyone donated them last year for the project. That's the great thing about the cougar community. Everyone helps out. I've got markers for drawing the faces, but we also have scraps of felt to use to create the faces—glue on or sew on."

"You have a sewing kit?"

"You bet. I know how to sew buttons or tears in clothing." He smiled at her.

She smiled. "Good. I'll sew on some faces."

Once all the pants and shirts were stuffed, they began to safety pin them together and tucked the "tail" of the pillowcase stuffed heads into the neck of the shirt. Then secured the heads to the necks of the shirts with safety pins.

She cut up some triangles to make eyes for some of the faces while Ted was creating other faces with marker.

Then he left the house and returned with a small bale of straw in a bucket. "We tuck these around the neck, leg, and shirt openings and glue them where necessary."

She helped him with that but paused to see the heroine in the movie thriller in a tight spot and had to see her get out of it. She'd been shot in the leg and had to take cover. Then someone was shooting from a different angle and everything went silent, until the heroine heard running footfalls headed in her direction. She raised her gun to shoot at the gunman when the hero called out to her, "Where are you, Sheri?"

"Russell!"

And then there was more gunfire.

Silence.

Stella was glued to the show now, unable to work on the scarecrow she'd been adding straw to until she learned how this turned out.

Then the heroine heard footfalls again, only this time, they sounded different. She didn't dare call out where she was again.

"It's me, Russell," the hero said, limping into view and she struggled to get up from where she was sitting.

"No, don't get up. We've got help coming."

Stella smiled. Then began working on the scarecrow again. "I love happy endings."

"Like yours."

She smiled at Ted. "Yeah, really nice to a rough beginning."

Once they had finished all ten scarecrows, Ted stacked them near the bookcases. "We'll put them up tomorrow, while you're back at your job, unless you change your mind and want to stay here another day."

"I'd love to, really. It's a catch-22. If I didn't heal so fast, I'd go in on Wednesday, and rest another day. But then my wounds wouldn't be as visible to my co-workers. If I go in tomorrow, they'll be more visible, but I'll be tired too. I might leave work a little early, if I get too worn out."

"That sounds like a good idea. Don't overdo it or you'll end up back in the clinic here. Though if you do, I'll bring you more flowers and bring you home-cooked meals, part of the Yuma Town clinic experience."

She laughed. "What if someone else is hospitalized and wants the same treatment?"

"I suspect I might be banned from the clinic."

She smiled. She really was enjoying being here with him and even doing the arts and crafts was a joy. She hadn't done anything like that in forever. She was glad she could make these with Ted.

They finished the movie then. He was going to grill steaks, a special send off before she returned home to Grand Junction. She had such mixed emotions about it. She truly wanted to just stay here and be with him at least for another day. But she knew, as addictive as he was, she'd want to stay another day, and another, until Friday came, and it was time for the Halloween party. And then what? Stay the weekend and then be feeling the same way about the next week? She had it in mind that maybe she'd get it out of her system. This need to be with other cougars. To be with Ted. That she was just tired from being injured. That once she was her normal self, she would be ready to return to doing her normal activities.

But she suspected spending a whole week with Ted wouldn't be enough, or that it would change her mind about being with him further. She couldn't stay here though. What about Kolby and the other ranch hands? They had to return to the bunkhouse. And then it wouldn't be the same—just her and Ted enjoying the house like it was their own. Besides, Ted had to get back to work and she knew she would be bored if she was just watching him work or sitting in the house curled up on the sofa, watching TV.

"Hey, after I start the steaks, do you want to make some pumpkin pie together? Do you even like pumpkin pie?"

"I do. I love pecan pie too."

"Okay, next time, we'll have a pecan pie." Once he started the steaks, he and Stella started working on the pumpkin pie.

She had already started on the pie crust and he smiled at it.

"Now that looks good," he said.

"It was one of the things my adoptive mother taught me how to do. Make pie crusts. And pies. It was the only kind of dessert she liked."

Then instead of him teaching her how to make a pie, he became her assistant, helping her with the pie filling and then he had to check on the steaks again. They soon sat down to eat and then he asked her, "Can you come early to the party on Friday?"

"I was thinking of that. So I could help out if anyone needed me to."

"Good. I will be anticipating your return all week."

She smiled. "At least it's a short week now. Just three days and a wake up. So what other crafty things do you make?" She was fascinated that he even made scarecrows and painted pumpkins. She would love to get into more craft work to give herself a hobby instead of just watching TV or reading books after work or on the weekends.

"Hmm, well, I've whittled a bit. And I help build the stone wall for Tracey's garden, because she wanted to keep the cows and horses out of her vegetables. The calves had sneaked under the fence to the pastureland and ended up in her garden one time, and she had a fit. I don't blame her. They pulled up all her vegetables and ate half of them."

"Oh, that would be frustrating."

"It was. So I was designated as the castle wall builder. Chase, whose ancestors built and maintained a castle in Scotland, helped me design it and build it. Though a lot of the guys ended up helping with the project, and we made a real celebration out of it. That's how we do things around here. The ladies brought us drinks and visited with each other. All the CSF agents, deputy sheriffs, sheriff, Kolby, they were involved in a lot of it. It took a lot of teamwork."

"That's what I would love to have around a garden. It makes it look like a country estate garden with the moss growing on the rocks in the shade, and the little rock sedums. So cute. I never would have imagined you and the others built it. I just figured some landscape company did it. That is so neat."

"Thanks. It turned out really well. The wrought iron gates leading into the garden were Chase's idea too, since they had those at the old Scottish estate."

"I love that."

After Ted and Stella finished dinner, it was time for her to drive home.

"Are you sure you don't want to stay at the ranch one more night?" he asked.

"No, I really feel fine and I don't have that much sick leave to use up."

"All right. Well, I can drive you home, while someone else drives your vehicle to your apartment."

"No, I can do it," Stella said to Ted, and she helped him clean up after the meal. She gave him a hug and a kiss after they were done. She knew he didn't want to see her go. She hadn't figured she would feel this way about a man so completely after knowing him for such a short time, but she really would miss his company and everyone else's once she returned home.

After one final kiss, she finally climbed into her Jeep and left to return to Grand Junction. When she reached home, she should have felt glad to be in her own little home. But it was dark and quiet and not half as nice as the bunkhouse. Her apartment looked over a parking lot and other parts of the complex. A pool and clubhouse were situated in the middle, but the pool was closed for the fall and it didn't appeal as much as the pond and the waterfall that she and Ted had ridden to by horseback.

Despite having been shot and bitten beforehand, the last couple of days had been magical. Still, she was looking forward to Halloween and couldn't wait to return to see the cougars—especially Ted, who made her melt in his arms.

CHAPTER 8

*W*hen Stella went to work on Tuesday morning, she hadn't wanted to say anything about what had happened to her and hoped no one else would bring it up.

"Did you have a nice three-day weekend?" Tori asked as if she really didn't believe Stella had been shot.

"Right." Getting shot twice didn't count as a fun three-day weekend, but Stella couldn't be gladder that she'd found so many new friends, cougar friends, to party with.

"So tell us what happened," Tori said.

Stella knew they didn't believe she'd been shot and bitten by a rattlesnake. How could she have been back to work this quickly? It was a good thing she still had the wounds to prove that she had, though they had healed up to some degree, much faster than if she'd been human. She pulled off her suit jacket and showed them her arm where she'd been shot twice. Even the lawyers came out of their offices to see her wounds. Then she sat down and lifted her pant leg to show them her snakebite.

"That's awful," Tori said, the others echoing her statement. "I can't believe you're back to work so soon."

"I'm just lucky I heal pretty quickly, or I wouldn't be."

One of the lawyers said to her, "Have the men responsible been charged for a crime against you?"

"Yes. They were shooting at the building I was in and they could have hit others at the ranch. They were hunters and guess who the one man was?" She told them about Jeffrey Sims. "The man you represented in court for illegal trespass and hunting."

The lawyer's face fell a little. Stella and the other paralegals loved their work when they were helping a lawyer protect someone who was being railroaded into pleading guilty of a crime. But in a case like Sims, they knew he would be the kind of man that would continue to do illegal hunting, figuring he could get away with it over and over again, as long as he always had a high-paid lawyer who was good at his job to represent him.

This time, she hoped the lawyers in the agency wouldn't represent him.

"If he gets away with shooting you, I'll represent you in a civil case," Kristy Brown said. "I won't be representing Sims or his buddies this time. I'm sorry to hear it. Are you doing okay?"

"Yeah, but it was frightening, and the men had shot up the place when there were four four-year olds in the yard. What kind of men do something like that? It's just a good thing that the walls of the barn helped to slow down the bullets so when they impacted with me"—which wasn't true at all—"they didn't do as much damage."

"Well, they'll have to seek someone else's representation this time."

That made Stella feel better. "Thanks. I appreciate that."

Then the lawyers and she got back to work, but during lunch break, Tori asked her, "So what were you doing in a barn at a horse ranch?"

"I had taken a horse ride earlier."

"Oh, no, were any of the horses injured?"

"No, thankfully." She'd never really thought out the consequences of her actions—of endangering the livestock, or people at the ranch when she headed for that barn. To her, that was her place of escape and she hadn't been able to think of anything else. Of course, she hadn't thought the men would shoot at anything other than her either.

"Oh, good. Because I know the prosecutor would prosecute this case, but if the ranch owners need civil representation also, our lawyers would certainly represent them."

"Thanks. I'm sure they would."

"Are you having nightmares about it?"

"Yeah. It's hard not to as the men riddled the barn with bullets. Thankfully, one of the men visiting the ranch happened to be an FBI agent. He was armed and shouting to them to drop their weapons and get on the ground."

"Oh, how awful."

No matter how bad the situation had been, life threatening for several of them, especially herself, at least she'd had a great story to tell about why she had taken a sick leave day for Monday.

"Wait, so why did they shoot up the barn? Were they pissed off at the rancher for some reason?"

This was the problem with telling the staff the real reason she had missed work yesterday. But she hadn't wanted to pretend she was just sick and couldn't make it in and then seemed perfectly healthy. She never did that in her life, and she wasn't going to now. But she knew, if they followed the news when they went to trial, the men would say they were shooting at a white cougar—which seemed ridiculous enough that maybe no one would believe them anyway. But it would come out—at least from their testimony, or their lawyers, if the men didn't take the stand and tell their own story in their defense.

"They said they'd shot a white cougar and they believed it had gone into the barn."

The other paralegals stopped their work to listen to her. One said, "No way. Were they drinking?"

"I don't know. All I know is that the ranch foreman who came to see to my injuries—to save my life—was yelling at them to throw down their weapons too. He had a rifle on him when he came into the barn to check on me."

"They knew you'd been shot already?"

"No, but Ted was afraid I might have been as many bullets as the hunters had fired at the building and through the open doors."

"Oh, I bet you were scared."

"Yeah, I managed to make it up a ladder into a hayloft. Truly, I don't even remember it. I just remember Ted coming to see me there."

"And the rattlesnake bite?" Tori asked.

"I don't remember exactly. I think it was in the barn when I went inside. I heard a rattle, and I knew there was a rattlesnake, but the men were shooting, and I was just trying to find cover."

"There isn't such a thing as a white cougar," one of the women said. "I mean, it says here on this website they're so rare, that I doubt that's what they saw."

"They claim they shot it. But there was no cougar in the barn and no wounded cougar anywhere on the acreage. The ranch hands and several people went out and looked. They intended to take care of it and put it in a cat reserve near there." She had to fabricate that part, but she knew of the cat reserve. She'd gone there a few times, hoping that if there ever was a cougar locked up in there who was truly a shifter, she could figure out a way to free him or her. She'd never had any indication one was, but it was just something she felt she needed to do because she'd hoped that if she had ever ended up in one, someone would do that for her.

"Could it have run off?" Tori asked.

"If it had been shot twice and bleeding the whole way that they said it had, probably not. He would have bled to death. Vultures would have circled the area if the cat had died or was near death somewhere. The ranch hands watched for any signs of it, but they didn't find a trail of blood, and no sign of vultures circling, indicating something had died."

"So the men had lied," Tori said.

"Or they were drunk. Who knows?"

"Oh, did they get a picture of it?" Tori asked.

"No. See, if I had seen a rare white cougar, I would have gotten a picture of it. Instead, what do they want to do?" Stella asked.

"Shoot it."

"Right. Then if they truly had seen a white cougar and killed it, they'd take pictures of the dead animal and share it all over," Stella said.

"Morbid."

"Exactly." If nothing else, maybe Stella could impress upon the ladies that the cougar could be a thing of beauty, not just a predator to kill.

"Did they kill the rattlesnake? The ranch hands?" Tori asked.

"Oh, I don't know. I never asked." Nope, the rattlesnake had only been protecting himself, and there wasn't any reason to kill it. "They might have rehomed it."

One of the women shivered. "Hate snakes."

"Think of it this way, if someone can capture it, they can have antivenom for someone who might need it later."

"True," Tori said.

Stella couldn't quit thinking of Ted though, and taking her for a fun horseback ride, playing with the kids, and she couldn't wait to go to the party.

"Hey, so some of us are going to a Halloween party on Friday night. Did you want to go to it?" Tori asked, changing the subject.

"I've got one to go to."

"Oh, who's hosting it? Maybe it would be more fun than the one I'm going to. Or I could go to both."

Stella shouldn't have mentioned it. "It's a by-invitation only."

"You leave for three days, get shot up, and come back with an invitation to a special event. So where is it being held?"

"Yuma Town."

"It's been a while since I drove through there. Who's giving the party?"

"The Havertons." Stella hoped Tori wouldn't ask her any more questions about it. It was an all-cougar event, and she was thrilled to be going to it, and it really was a private event, by-invitation only. Then she had a notification on her phone showing that she had a package.

She glanced at the email.

"What's that?" Tori asked.

Stella showed her the email that had a picture of the item she had ordered. The beautiful gown for the western-themed Halloween party.

"Ohmigod, that's beautiful. Not a vampire and witch affair, then."

"No, it's my favorite party theme too."

"Oh, yeah, I know. You want to watch westerns mostly. That's okay, I'm going as a witch to the Halloween party I've been invited to. You can still come if you want. And be the belle of the party." Tori smiled, then answered the phone for work.

By lunchtime, Stella had received ten messages from Ted, all photos of the activities they'd participated in that she hadn't realized anyone was taking pictures of—her riding Celestina, the beautiful appaloosa with the white bottom and chestnut colored body and spots all over her backside. She was such a sweet horse and Stella loved that Ted had picked her out of the stable of horses to ride for the very first time.

Then he'd taken a picture of her watching the waterfall, and she hadn't realized he'd taken that either. One of the nurses had snapped a shot of them leaving the clinic as if to commemorate their time together, which Stella thought was sweet.

She noticed no one had taken a picture of her as a wounded white cougar, and she was glad for that.

* * *

WHEN STELLA WENT HOME that night, all she could think of was Ted grilling steaks for them, roasting marshmallows at sunset, and hearing the owls hoot off in the woods and how much she missed being with him. And being shot at by hunters while running as a cougar!

Ted sent another text as she was getting ready to make herself a grilled chicken sandwich for dinner: *Missing you terribly. I didn't realize we were being documented together, except for the one photo I took of you at the waterfalls. But I wanted to share them with you.*

She texted back: *I'm missing you too. It's not the same being here at my apartment now that I'm all alone. I had such a wonderful time with you at the bunkhouse and everything we did together. I can't believe I forgot to say goodbye to Celestina when I left.*

Ted: *I'll give her an apple and say it's from you. I wish you were here too.*

She smiled and texted: *It's a deal.*

He texted: *How did things go at work for you today?*

Stella: *Oh, no one believed I had been shot. I mean, it wasn't that they thought I out and out lied about it, but there was nothing in any news reports about it—everyone had looked when I called in sick—and of course they were curious how bad the injuries were. So that meant I had to show them off to satisfy their curiosity.*

Ted: *And they finally believed you.*

Stella: *Yeah. And I'm sure they felt guilty if they had some notion I had just made up a wallop of a story to have a three-day vacation.*

Ted: *We decided not to put the news in the local paper because we don't want to have droves of people coming here, looking for a dead white cougar. We'll try to keep the lid on the story about the white cougar and just say the men were shooting at a cougar.*

Stella: *Okay, good. How are things going on the Halloween party preparations?*

Ted: *Good. It's a lot of work but I'm sure you'll really enjoy it. Let me know if you want me to pick you up and take you there. How are you feeling? I should have asked that of you first thing.*

Stella: *Good. A little sore. I won't be running as a cougar for the rest of the week, though maybe by Friday I could do it.*

Ted: *Only if you're here with us.*

Stella: *Yes! I'm not going to look for a new place to run for now.*

Ted: *Kolby's made us dinner, so I'm going to go eat with him. But I just wanted to check on you, send the pictures, and make sure everything's okay at work.*

She smiled and texted: *Thanks. It is. And thanks for the pictures. Night, Ted. See you soon.*

CHAPTER 9

ith all the texts Ted had sent Stella, he hoped she wouldn't think he was bugging her all the time while she was back in Grand Junction, but he couldn't help himself.

He had an important mission today. He had to go in and talk to Larry Pierce about drawing up a will to give everything he owned, should he die, to his niece and nephew and grand nephews. But he had an ulterior motive too. He had to find a job for Stella so she could live in Yuma Town and be among their kind.

As soon as he went into the office that located between the bank and the newspaper office, he saw Roberta Barrington, Larry's receptionist, on the phone and she smiled and motioned for him to take a seat.

Normally, Ted figured the lawyer wouldn't be that busy with business here in Yuma Town, no one seemed to get divorced, no custody cases, but a lot of folks had been going to Loveland for other legal business and so Larry was swamped.

"He has got you down for your appointment," she said to Ted, "but he's got a potential client calling from jail and he needed to speak with him."

"Sure, no problem." Then Ted frowned. "From our jail? Yuma Town? You mean Jeffrey Sims and his buddies?"

"Yeah, I know." Roberta rolled her eyes. "Mr. Pierce won't take the case, you know, but he had to take the call. If he took the case, he would make sure they didn't get a finding of innocent. In fact, he said he's ready to take Stella White's case concerning them to trial in civil court."

"That's good news. Actually, I came to speak to him about Stella also."

"Oh." Roberta smiled. "Good. Larry, uhm, Mr. Pierce is so grateful to be here, he wants to prove to the community that he'll protect us like no other lawyer can."

"Actually, I wanted to talk to him about hiring Stella on as a paralegal."

Roberta's eyes widened. "Oh, yes, he so needs a trained paralegal. Stella's one? I've been muddling through for him, but really, all I can do is take phone calls and I've been managing his finances and filing for him. Which is a lot, actually, but the other stuff? A paralegal needs to do the research and filing motions and stuff like that." Then she smiled. "You want to date her. You are dating her. My brother told me you were. Jack said you were the first one to give her emergency medical aid."

"Yeah, I'm dating her. But she needs to be with us, with the cougar community. And she needs to be employed by another cougar. The whole set up couldn't be more perfect."

"I'll say. Poor Mr. Pierce is just swamped. He had a paralegal all lined up to come down here—she's a cougar who was working in the human legal firm he was working at in Denver. But she got cold feet. I think her family didn't want her to move so far away. Anyway, so when she backed out, he had to go on his own, and he thought maybe eventually I could get the training to be a paralegal, but it would take so much time. He really needs one now."

The phone rang and she had to answer it.

Then Larry stepped out of his office and motioned Ted to come into his office. "How's Ms. White doing?"

"She was feeling well enough to return to Grand Junction to work for Brown and Sons."

"The legal firm?" Larry asked, taking a seat while Ted sat in a leather chair across from his hardwood desk.

"Yeah, she's a paralegal with Brown and Sons, and I wanted to see if you were in need of one."

"Oh, yeah, I sure am. I'm just swamped with work to do. I never figured I'd be this busy." Larry smiled. "But I'm glad to be as long as I can help my fellow cougars out. Was she inquiring about a position with me?"

"Uh, no, but I wanted to see if you even needed anyone, before I talked with her about it."

"Ah, you want to date her."

"I'm dating her." Ted wanted everyone to know that!

Larry smiled again. "Yes, I would love to have her work for me. And I still intend to talk to her about making a civil case against the men who shot her. Ballistics haven't come back to prove which man, or if more had done the deed, but they were all shooting, so they're all culpable. And there will be no charge to her for my services."

Ted nodded. "I'm sure she will be glad to hear the news." Now if only he could convince her she needed to work for Larry Pierce.

"Okay, thanks. If you need me to call her up and beg for her to come work for me, just let me know. Roberta can tell you I'm a nice guy to work for."

"He is," Roberta called out, "and I'm not just saying that to keep my job."

Ted chuckled.

"You said you needed an updated will."

"Yeah." Of course if Ted ended up mating with Stella, it would have to be updated again, which was another good reason for having a lawyer right here in town. "The last time I had one done in Loveland, my other nephew wasn't married. They're expecting twins in the spring. I want to include them too, in addition to my niece and my grand-nephews."

"I can take care of that right away."

Ted handed him the old will and began filling him in on details of how things needed to be set up.

He was feeling good about talking to Larry about hiring Stella. He just hoped she wouldn't be annoyed with him for doing so without talking to her first. But he felt it would have been foolish to mention her working for Larry Pierce if he hadn't been interested in hiring her, either because he already had a paralegal coming to work for him, or because he just didn't need one. What did he know? He was glad Larry did need one and that both he and Roberta were eager to have Stella work in his office.

"Oh, and thanks for not taking on Jeffrey Sims' and his buddies' case," Ted said.

"Yeah, that would be business suicide for me if I had. And my sister and brother-in-law would disown me." Larry shook his head. "Not that I would ever take a case where I would have to defend a human hunter shooting any of our kind. There could be a case, if I thought about it hard enough, where a cougar was at fault, but I just couldn't do it. Not to mention I was there when all the shooting was going on and so was a witness." Larry let out his breath. "Which means I couldn't be Stella's lawyer in a civil case either. But maybe her current employer would do so."

If she was working for Larry by then, maybe not. "Did you ever have to handle a rogue cougar case in Denver?"

"No. Those of us who are shifters stayed out of trouble. If any had done some major crime, I would have called on a CSF agent to deal with it and move the cougar out of our jurisdiction so he, or she, wouldn't be in our prison system. Too scary to think of the consequences of that."

"I agree with you there."

Once the legal documents were prepared, Ted signed them and the lawyer signed them, and then he got a copy and Roberta filed the other. "Thanks, Mr. Pierce."

"Larry, please. We're all like family here and I'd like to keep it that way."

Ted shook his hand. "Larry then."

Roberta got a call and said, "That's for you, Mr. Pierce."

Then Ted was out the door and headed back to the ranch. He thought he would wait until tonight to call Stella with the job opportunity. He didn't want to interrupt her work and he didn't want to text her when he was afraid she might be annoyed with him. So he needed to talk to her upfront about it.

It was lunchtime when he arrived home and he was glad Kolby had made lunch for them. He smelled the spicy, sausage spaghetti as soon as he walked in the door. He loved Kolby's spaghetti.

"Thanks for making lunch for us." Ted hung up his Stetson.

"No problem. I know how much you like it." Kolby set the plates of spaghetti on the table. He had learned to cook and take care of his younger brother, Ricky, which made it nice because Ted and Kolby switched off on cooking meals. "You know, you remind me of a lovesick pup."

Smiling, Ted set the silverware on the table.

"I've never seen you texting like it was going out of style." Kolby took his seat at the table and Ted joined him.

"I was sending Stella photos that everyone took of her and of us." Speaking of which, he needed to take pictures of Celestina and send them to Stella for the rest of the week.

Kolby forked up some of his spaghetti. "Ahh. Did it convince her that she needed to return here sooner than later?"

"I hope everything I do will."

"See, that's what I said. You're like a lovesick pup."

"Tomorrow—" Then Ted thought better of it. He would ask Tracey to help him out.

"Tomorrow, what?" Kolby asked, his interest piqued.

"Nothing." Ted wished he hadn't brought it up.

"What?" Kolby wasn't letting it go.

"I want someone to take a picture of me feeding Celestina an apple."

Kolby looked puzzled for a minute. Then he smiled. "Stella rode Celestina with you and Pablo to the waterfalls. She's missing the horse? Not you?" He laughed.

"She regretted not saying goodbye to her before she left. So I told her"—though Ted didn't know why he was telling Kolby all this—"that I'd give Celestina and apple for her. And it wouldn't be the same if I didn't actually send a picture of Celestina—"

"And you."

"—feeding her the apple." Ted took a bite of the spaghetti.

"Right. Sure, I'll do it unless you think Tracey would take a better picture."

"You can do it. The kids would probably want in the picture and then it would be a shot of all the kids and the horse and that might not be as conducive to convincing Stella she wants to be here."

"Permanently." Kolby smiled.

"This is great, by the way. Your spaghetti is always the best."

"Thanks. That's why I always make it. I'm making the pirate spaghetti for the Halloween party too."

"I can't wait to see how that turns out."

"So when do you want me to take a picture of you feeding Celestina an apple?" Kolby asked.

"After dinner."

Kolby smiled.

Ted shrugged. "That way Stella can sleep well, knowing Celestina got her apple from her."

Kolby chuckled. "All right. Hey, did you talk to the lawyer about hiring Stella when you went in to change your will? I hope you did. I heard that he had a paralegal hired to do the job and then all of a sudden, she changed her mind. You didn't have anything to do with it, did you?"

Ted laughed. "No, but I'm glad it happened if Stella wants the job. According to Roberta and Larry, the paralegal from Denver had family up there and they convinced her not to move to some out-of-the-way place like Yuma Town, even though we're cougar run. I'm sure they worried she'd meet someone and then end up mating him and not wanting to leave. And the family didn't want to have to move here to see her. Anyway, yeah, I talked to Larry about the job and he definitely wants to hire her. So I just need to talk to Stella about it tonight."

"It's the other paralegal cougar's loss. Though, come to think of it, what if I'd had a chance to date her? Stella's for sure already taken." Kolby shook his head.

Yeah, that was for certain, Ted thought, if he had any say in it.

CHAPTER 10

$\mathcal{S}$tella was researching the background of a client her boss was representing when Ms. Brown came out to speak with her. "Jeffrey Sims called to tell us that he needed representation for a shooting incident at a horse ranch near Yuma Town. The one you were involved in."

Stella practically held her breath. She couldn't imagine the lawyers from this firm would represent the bastards.

"I didn't take the case," Ms. Brown assured her. "I told him it would be a conflict of interest because the victim, whom they shot, works for me. Then he proceeded to tell me you had been trespassing illegally on the Havertons' ranch, but we know that isn't true since you went horseback riding there, according to your own testimony."

"Right." Though not before the shooting, of course. And cougars running on the property would never have been considered "trespassing."

"I just wanted to warn you that they could end up getting another lawyer to represent them and he might be able to release them on bail."

"What? They shot me!"

"I know, but when we researched their background—well, you did—for the previous charges they'd incurred for trespassing and illegally hunting, you couldn't find anything on the men that would indicate they had been convicted of any criminal charges before that."

Yeah, Stella couldn't. But that didn't mean they hadn't done a bunch of illegal stuff. Just that they'd never been caught at it or been convicted of the crime—because they'd never been convicted of criminal charges before that!

She'd still believed a judge wouldn't release the men because they'd shot her!

When Ms. Brown returned to her office, Tori said to Stella, "I love working here, but I hate when scumbags get off just because they have a good lawyer."

"Yeah, if I had pulled that, I'd probably be locked up for good," Stella said, still furious at the thought, but she was hoping the judge who listened to the case would be smart about it and keep the men in jail until their trial.

* * *

TED WAS BREAKING a horse when he got a call from Dan and left the corral to take the call. He figured it was important, or the sheriff wouldn't be trying to get in touch with him. "Yeah, Dan?"

"Hey, I have some bad news for you and Stella. Jeffrey Sims and his buddies got some fancy lawyer out of Denver to represent them and they had the hearing and the judge set the bail at five thousand apiece. They're all out on bail."

"Hell."

"Yeah, that's how we feel. Both their lawyer and the judge are hunters, so not good for our side. But I needed to tell you and Hal and Tracey, just in case the bastards return to cause trouble at the ranch or lands around it, looking for the wounded or dead white cougar."

It always pissed Ted off when men could get out of jail on bond after shooting someone! Even though they thought they were shooting at a cougar, they could have hit someone else in the barn, if someone else had been in it, and everyone else who'd been out in the yard at the time. Would the lawyer and the judge get them off because they were fellow hunters? Damn it!

"Hey, they're not getting off this time. And I'm sure no judge in his right mind would find in favor of the hunters," Dan said, trying to reassure him. "I spoke with Larry about it and he said the same thing. It could have been anyone in the barn, the kids, a whole family, not just one person who had been shot."

They spoke about it so much as if the men had truly hit Stella as a human in the barn and not while running as a cougar on the cliffs, that he was almost believing it himself.

"We've got extra patrols going on around the ranch and the area where Stella was shot, but everyone in the community is being warned about the men. The thing is, they're dangerous for any of us, if any of us go running and the hunters decide to shoot another cougar—just to do it and try and get away with it," Dan said.

"I agree. No ankle monitor?" Ted figured they didn't have if Dan was afraid they'd come out to the ranch again.

"Nope. The judge didn't consider the men flight risks."

"I wouldn't really have considered them flight risks either. More that they would go out and illegally shoot more animals on private property is all. Thanks for letting me know. I'll tell Stella."

Ted hated calling Stella about the bad news—that Sims and his buddies were free to walk the streets again, but he could hardly wait to tell her that she could have a new job as a paralegal in Yuma Town, and he prayed she would take it.

"Hey, Stella, I have good news and bad news," he said to her that night after work.

"Don't tell me. Sims and the others are out on bail," Stella said.

She must have already gotten word. He wished he'd been there for her when she had.

"My boss said that he tried to hire her for the job to represent him because she had before and gotten him off. So he figured she was a sure bet. She told him no, because I worked for her and there would be a conflict of interest. But she told me that some other lawyer would probably be able to get him out on bail."

"I'm so sorry. Dan called me right away, and wanted me to tell you, but I wanted to wait until you got off work."

"Don't be sorry. It's not your fault. It makes me angry, but there's nothing any of us can do about it." She let out her breath. "So what's the good news?"

At least he hoped Stella would think it was good news. "You have an offer to work at a paralegal job for Larry Pierce in Yuma Town." Ted couldn't think of any better news than that.

"The ambulance chaser?"

"Huh?"

"Sorry. When he came to tell me he'd take my case after I was shot and still in my cougar form, that's what I was thinking of. He was an ambulance chaser."

Ted chuckled. "Oh, okay. No. I mean, I don't think he is. He just started working in Yuma Town and I chanced to go in to update my will and—"

"You learned he was looking for a paralegal?"

"Yeah. Roberta Barrington is working as his secretary and financial officer, but she can't do the paralegal work. The office where you work probably has a ton of paralegals and they could afford to lose you, whereas Larry doesn't have anyone, and he's swamped with work."

"It doesn't mean he wants to hire me, in particular."

"Oh, yeah, he does. I'm supposed to beg you, or he'll call and beg you. We need a cougar paralegal and—"

"You want to date me."

He smiled. "Hell, yeah. So is that good news, or are you mad at me for bringing it up to Larry?"

"Wait, you didn't actually just learn there was a need for one?"

Okay, so he shouldn't have mentioned that part. "Uh, well, I just mentioned it to Roberta, and she was all over it, saying yes! You needed to work with them. And, she totally vouched for Larry, saying he was great to work for. And then when I mentioned it to Larry, he was eager to hire you. He also said he would have represented you in a civil case against the hunters, but then recalled he would be a witness at the criminal trial and a civil trial, if you take it that far."

"Oh. He was a witness?"

"Yeah, he was helping get Tracey's kids to safety."

"So not an ambulance chaser."

Ted chuckled. "I don't know about that, but he even makes house calls for some of his legal business and he asked first thing about how you were doing, before he knew you were a paralegal or anything."

"Okay."

"So you'll take the job? Please say yes."

She laughed. "I have to think on it. You just hit me with the notion of quitting my job, working for another lawyer—"

"Who's a cougar."

"And moving to Yuma Town."

"All of us will help with it."

She sighed. "I need to think on it. I need to know if the pay is commensurate with what I earn now. If the other benefits—health and sick leave, paid vacation days—are similar to what I get now."

"He'll better it. I'm sure of it. Like I said, he has no one working for him now, well, except the receptionist, but no paralegal, so you have him at an advantage."

She chuckled. "Okay, well, let me think about it."

He sighed. "All right. You think on it." He gave her Larry's number and the location of his office. "Are you all right being alone tonight? I mean, as far as Sims and his buddies being out on bail."

"Yeah, as long as I don't run as a cougar in Grand Junction, I should be all right. And...thanks, Ted, for trying to get me a job in Yuma Town."

"That's good news, isn't it?"

She laughed and then they talked and finally ended the call so they could retire to bed.

So what did that mean? Was it good news or not?

* * *

THE NEXT MORNING, Stella woke and had three texts from Ted already. She chuckled as she made her hot tea. One was of Celestina eating an apple, and another was of Celestina and Pablo nuzzling each other. The last was a text from Ted saying: *Good morning! How are you doing? Feeling okay?*

She smiled and ate a scrambled egg, slice of toast, and two sausage links.

She texted him back: *Feeling great. You're not worried I'm going to change my mind about coming to the party, are you?*

You're not, are you?

No way. I have my gown. This will be my first function to attend that's cougar run so I'll get to meet all kinds of cougars.

Ted texted: *Do you think you might want to work for Larry Pierce?*

Stella pulled on her pumps and then her suit jacket.

Ted texted: *He's from Denver and was with a first-class firm there.*

She didn't say anything. She didn't know what to say.

She texted back: *I'm still thinking about it. I'm off to work. I'll talk to you later.*

Then she went to work and wondered if that would work out. It would mean living in a cougar community, which was great news. But she really loved the lawyers she worked for here.

Would she even like Larry Pierce at all? She couldn't imagine moving from a job she loved to one she hated. Not all lawyers were equal. Then again, her social life would increase exponentially, and she really did like the idea of that.

She walked into the office and it wasn't long before she received another bouquet of white roses.

The paralegals all raised brows and smiled at her.

"I could use a lover boy like that," Tori said.

Yeah, that was really what Stella was thinking. It wasn't just that she could have a job or the social engagements with other cougars, though that helped to convince her to move, but it was Ted—his smiles, his helpfulness and his protectiveness, his interest in her, his romantic nature, and how caring he was. She loved how he was with the animals, with the kids, with people in general. It was uplifting to be with him in any setting. Yet when it came to the bad guys, he was all cougar gruff, ready to tear into them and protect the innocent.

But she had to wait until the party and see if what she was feeling, this longing and need to be with him and the other cougars would still be there. That it wasn't just something she had dreamed up because she'd been filled with drugs and even when she'd come off them, that she wasn't feeling a sense of belonging because everyone was concerned about just her health.

She received ten more texts from Ted throughout the day—videos of him breaking a new horse, taking the kids for a ride, one at a time, petting Celestina and telling her that Stella would be returning soon and would ride her when she could. That brought tears to Stella's eyes.

Ted was such a sweetheart. She couldn't show him pictures of anything fun at her work and she loved that he would share what she enjoyed, his cowboy world, with her.

"What's he texting you about now?" Tori asked, coming to check the pictures out.

This time, Stella let her see them.

"Oh, man, he's hot."

Then the other paralegals had to come over and see the videos too.

They smiled. "You have a real catch there," one of the paralegals said.

Yeah, that's the way Stella was feeling too.

That night, she returned to her apartment and here came her roses, and also more text messages. They made her feel not half as lonely and connected to him too.

But then he called her. "Hey, I've been missing you," Ted said.

"Yeah, I feel the same way about you." She couldn't stop thinking about cuddling with him on the couch while watching a movie, the fire crackling in the fireplace, rain pouring overhead. It was romantic and homey, something she hadn't felt in a good long while.

"Are you sure you're all right alone? I feel awful about the guys getting out of jail."

"Yeah, sure. I'll be fine."

"Are you sure? Dan, our sheriff, said he can send one of our deputies to watch over you at night. Hal said he'd been the first one on the list to do so."

She smiled. "No. That's all right. I'll be there in a couple of days' time to enjoy the party with you."

"Okay, well, you call me if you have any trouble at all, in the middle of the night or any other time. I'll be there."

But he still lived an hour away, so she would be better off just calling the local police. Though working for a law firm sometimes worked against her. The police detectives would hand over evidence to the prosecutor and expect the crime to be prosecuted in their favor, and then her bosses would get the man, or woman, who was charged, off on all charges. Not always, but a lot of times. But the police officers and detectives had to realize that if they were charged with a crime, the lawyers would be there to protect their rights too.

"Celestina is missing you," Ted said.

She laughed. As if the horse would even remember her.

"I show her pictures of you every day and she always nuzzles them with her nose."

Looking for food, no doubt.

"I can't wait to ride her again." She couldn't wait to do a lot of things with Ted again, she realized. Even running as a cougar, now that she was healing up nicely. She sighed. She really couldn't quit thinking about him either. Though some of that was because he texted her so much. But still, she enjoyed the little notes, videos, and pictures he sent her. She hadn't ever had anyone that interested in her that she was just as intrigued with. "All right, so did Larry Pierce need me to send my resume to him or had he planned to hire me sight unseen?"

"He wants to hire you no matter what. But it wouldn't hurt for you to send him your resume." He sounded hopeful that she was going to actually take the job.

She was really leaning toward taking the job. As a cougar, who wouldn't want to join the cougar community in the first place? Especially when the lawyer who wanted to hire her desperately needed her, so she would have a job even, which was really important to her. She'd been so used to nobody needing her in their lives—her own family especially—boyfriends, that she needed to just jump at the opportunity.

"I'll send it right away. And thanks, Ted, for wanting me to move out there to be with other cougars."

"And date me. I have to mention that because I really want us to see more of each other. Hell, if you'd been here, we would have had dinner out, movies out, cougar runs, horseback rides, you name it."

She was feeling worn out already.

"And just quiet time too," he quickly said.

She needed the quiet time with him too.

But the issue with the hunters was another good reason to

think about moving to Yuma Town. If she had any trouble at all, especially since she was a white cougar and might bring attention to herself sometime on a run as a cougar, she would be right there where others could help her. Here, she was an hour away from help from her kind.

They finally ended the call, and she was glad she had Ted's friendship that she knew was developing into so much more.

He sent more pictures of him feeding an apple to Celestina though, and she was looking forward to when she could do it too. She sent off her resume to Larry Pierce also, just in case this really might come to fruition. She wasn't about to give up her job though, until she knew for sure if she had another one she could begin working at.

* * *

THE NEXT DAY, Larry called Stella back about her resume while she was at work and she was trying not to let on to anyone that she had a new job offer. "Hi, this is Larry Pierce, and I'd like to tell you you're hired if you can start work right away. As soon as you give two-weeks' notice at your work."

But she still needed to know about the pay and other benefits. Though she figured living in the cougar town and dating Ted would make a big difference too. Still, she wanted to be paid for her work and didn't want to have her wages cut back. She really didn't want to talk about it in front of the other paralegals though. They were busy, but if she started talking about pay and such, she could just imagine all their attention being on her. And she sure didn't want to let the cat out of the bag until she was truly ready to give notice.

She said, "Uhm..."

"Pay and benefits. So I know you're at work, but I wanted to make sure I could entice you to work for me before I drown in work here and I could really use your help. You have an excellent resume, I'm impressed. That you're a cougar like me, I'm hiring. But I know you need to ensure your pay is commiserate with what you're already earning, and you probably don't want to discuss it over the phone. I assume you're making about 51K. Right?"

"Yes." Fifty and some change.

"I'll make it 60K."

Her jaw dropped. Tori raised her brows. Stella said, "Okay."

"As to time off—any time you need off, you've got it, as long as I don't have a major case going to trial that I need your help with. And you won't have to take vacation time for that. But you also will have a bonus every year, depending on the payout of cases, and three weeks paid vacation, and I will supplement your health insurance. Since we don't have long-lasting health issues as cougars, I don't expect you to need more than twenty days paid sick leave, but if you do, you'll have it. And I'll give you maternity leave when the time comes. Paid three months. I need you. I want you to work for me. You can give me your answer at the party."

She smiled. She wanted to just say yes! But she did want to meet him first. She didn't get bonuses here, and she only had two weeks paid vacation. He sounded like a dream boss to work for. She just hoped it wasn't a delusion.

"Okay, thanks." This could be the best thing that ever happened to her in whole entire life. But still, she wanted to make sure she wasn't kidding herself about what she was—a rare white cougar among a sea of normal, tan cougars.

She was thrilled, scared, excited, not sure if she was jumping the gun or what. "Thanks, I'll be at the Halloween party tomorrow—"

"I'll be there and come looking for you, then we can shake on it and you can give notice at your work after that."

Perfect. Because she wanted to see everyone at the party first, to ensure she wasn't making a big mistake in uprooting herself and moving to Yuma Town, though she was thrilled with the prospect.

"I look forward to seeing you there," she said, and they ended the call.

Tori was eyeing her with suspicion, but Stella couldn't share a thing about it. Not until she was ready to give notice for certain on Monday.

* * *

ONCE TED SPOKE to Larry Pierce about hiring Stella, just in case he was still considering it, Larry said he'd been swamped with a case, trying to do all the work a paralegal would do and his job too. So he sounded like he really needed her and wanted her, but he hadn't had time even to call her back with the news. Still, Ted had to leave him to it and not tell Stella the good news, if Larry changed his mind. Ted sure hoped not. He was an affable man, but who knew how he would be to work for. Ted just hoped he wasn't making a mistake as a go between for the two of them.

If things worked out between him and Stella, he was going to buy Celestina from Hal and Tracey and give the appaloosa to Stella for a wedding present. He just hoped she was thinking along the same lines as he was. Then again, maybe she wasn't as interested in the horse as he thought she was.

He had sent the horse statue to her office so she could show off that she had a boyfriend who was really into this business of courtship big time.

She called him right away. "Ohmigod, Ted, the horse is adorable. She is on permanent display on my desk. She's just adorable."

He hoped she would be on permanent display on Stella's desk in Yuma Town before long. He wanted to ask if Larry had called her yet, but he stifled the urge. "You haven't had any trouble with the hunters, have you?"

"No, if they did, you would be the first to know. Well, after the police. Since they're closer. But you know what I mean."

"Good. Anytime day or night, you let me know if you have any trouble with them."

"I will."

Then he had to let her go and he knew if she took the job here, he wouldn't be hassling her all the day long because he'd have her at home at night with him, if he could get her to agree and he could even have lunches with her and, well, hell, he was going to have to damn well mate her so he wouldn't feel driven to constantly text her and call on her to make sure she was all right.

He was working hard at the ranch, so it wasn't like he didn't have important stuff to do, but as soon as he had a moment, he had his phone out and he was texting her again. Kolby was ribbing him about it mercilessly in the beginning, but by the end of the week, he'd given up on it. Tracey and Hal were just amused.

By Friday, Ted had cleaned up his bedroom, getting it ready for her to stay, and he hoped she would spend the whole weekend with him. He also had bought some more roses for her that he had sitting on the dining room table.

He'd spent tons of time working at his regular chores, but also on the Halloween party decorations, setting out tables for the food and for everyone to sit down and eat at. And tons of chairs. He'd helped to get the band stage set up, and the dance floor too. Yet his mind was still on seeing Stella and making her feel welcome in what he hoped would soon be her new home.

He was even wearing his party Stetson and dance cowboy boots, new jeans and vest and western shirt just for her when she finally arrived.

CHAPTER 11

*O*n Friday, Stella was excited for the week to finally end when she drove to the Havertons' ranch for the Halloween party, feeling both thrilled and apprehensive. She had left early from work so she could help with whatever needed doing.

Even though she'd met some of the cougars of Yuma Town, she would meet so many more. Would the fun she'd had with Ted be the stuff of dreams or reality? She was afraid she'd built this all up in her mind so much, she hadn't really been seeing the truth of what she'd experienced. That everyone was so nice to her because she'd been wounded and after she was fine, everything would be different.

That was the problem with the way she'd always been treated as a white cougar. She didn't want to think that way about anyone in Yuma Town but that was always a concern for her.

As soon as she'd gotten her dress in for the western-themed party, she'd tried it on and hoped that Ted loved her in it as much as she loved the dress. She was glad she did and planned to dress at the main house or bunkhouse when it was time for the party to start.

All she could think of was seeing Ted again, but she hadn't made it very far down the road when she heard the telltale sound of one of her tires going flat, flapping, the drag on the pavement. *Great, just great.* At least she wasn't wearing her beautiful gown, just jeans, a warm, blue fleece jacket, and her brand-new cowgirl boots. She pulled the Jeep off the side of the road and got out her jack and the spare tire. She was glad she'd had a boyfriend a couple of years ago who had at least showed her how to change out a tire, though she supposed she could have called road service this time. Still, she was afraid it would take too long for someone to come and change her tire.

She was starting to jack up her car when she saw a pickup slowing down and pull off on the shoulder of the road. She didn't like the look of this at all. It looked suspiciously like Sims driving the truck.

And yeah, as soon as she removed the flat tire, Sims got out of the truck and sauntered over, in no hurry to help her, his buddies—the same ones with him when they shot her—came over too.

Her skin prickled with unease, as if a million nettles suddenly had pricked her, the chilly breeze whipping her hair about and she tried to keep it out of her eyes while she put the spare tire on the Jeep.

"Need some help, Miss White?" Sims said. "White, isn't it? One of the paralegals at Brown and Sons? You know, I figured Brown would be an old man, and his grown sons would be working there. Imagine my surprise when I learned that Mom was the lawyer, and the sons were her boys."

Even though Sims had asked her if Stella needed help, he wasn't making any overture to step in and do anything and she figured he really hadn't intended to help her.

She wished they would just leave her in peace. She didn't have a good feeling about them approaching her here like this and she wondered if they had anything to do with her tire going flat in the first place. Or was she just being paranoid about them being anywhere near her right now?

A couple of cars passed them by, shaking her vehicle, and she put the lug nuts on and tightened them.

"You know those people out at the ranch said you were shot in that barn."

She noticed he didn't say that *he* had done the shooting. Of course she didn't know whose bullets actually hit her either. Forensics would have to prove who had shot her. She'd been too busy trying to hide as a cougar at the time.

"But we can't figure that out. We were shooting at a white cougar," Clayton said.

"Yeah, it came at us. We had the right to defend ourselves," Sims said. "Your vehicle was parked near ours. So how in the hell did you end up in the barn where you were said to have been shot."

"Allegedly, right, Sims?" Clayton asked.

"Yeah, allegedly. And the cougar we shot was not on the Haverton's property either," Clayton said. "It jumped the fence."

"So it was just chasing you on the other side of the fence," Stella said, knowing she should have just kept her mouth shut.

"Yeah, that was the thing of it," Sims said.

She finished with the spare tire and carried the flat tire to the trunk of the Jeep, lifted it and dropped it inside, then shut the door.

"So how did you manage to get from your Jeep all the way to the barn?" Sims asked.

She smiled at them and then climbed into her Jeep and drove off. She could have made up a story, but she didn't need to, and she hadn't been about to and then have some lawyer question her about it. All that mattered when it went to trial was that she had been in the barn and they had shot her. And for now, she was going to a Halloween party with a bunch of cougars. Yet she couldn't help but watch the men driving behind her, not speeding up to pass her, or slowing down, but staying right behind her.

Trying to intimidate her? She wasn't easily intimidated unless she was being shot at when she was a cougar.

She still wondered if they had done something to her tire when she was parked at work or her apartment, though she hadn't remembered smelling their scent around her car. She figured if she had gotten a whiff of them, she would have been wary all at once. That was one thing about being a cougar. Her sense of smell was good enough that even after a rain, she could follow someone's scent trail.

She thought about calling Ted concerning the men following her, but she didn't want to ruin the party when she was sure he was busy helping out and as long as she didn't have any trouble with the men, there was no sense in creating a scene. Every mile she drove, she was getting closer to the ranch anyway.

She could just imagine Ted getting into a confrontation with the men and then real trouble starting. Forget about having a good time for either of them at the party then.

Though she felt uncomfortable with Sims following so close behind her. When she finally turned off on the road to the ranch, the men stopped following her, as if they knew they would face a bunch of guns again if they pulled anything around there. She needed to have her tire fixed too before she returned home. She had brought an overnight bag with some items for the weekend and another pair of shoes with her—really comfortable shoes, knowing she'd have to break in her cowgirl boots—if she wasn't being too forward and Ted wanted her to stay. Or she hadn't changed her mind about him either. Not that she thought she would. All she'd thought about was being with him again.

She was glad when the men headed back the way they had come and she knew then they were hassling her, certainly not giving her a safe escort to the ranch. She thought maybe she ought to come up with a story of why her Jeep was parked off the ranch property and she had been so far from there when she was in the barn. She would see what Ted thought might make a reasonable story that all parties could agree to. She certainly didn't want to get caught up in a lie.

Then she pulled onto the ranch and parked near some other cars where people had gathered for the party. She saw Ted right away, watching her, as if he had been doing nothing all this time but waiting for her.

She smiled at him, soured about the men hassling her, but thrilled to see Ted again, who brightened her spirits all at once.

Ted whooped when he saw her arrive, grinning from ear to ear, and hurried to open her Jeep door for her. She smiled at him, glad he was so enthusiastic about her coming. He carried her gown and instead of giving her a choice, he took her hand and walked her straight to the bunkhouse as if that's where she was supposed to go. "You can change in here," he said, putting it in his bedroom.

But once he had set the gown on the bed, he pulled her into his arms and kissed her like he thought he would never see her again and had to make sure she knew just how much it meant to him that she was there.

She wrapped her arms around Ted's neck and pressed her body against his body, eager to feel his hotness nice and close. "I missed you."

"Hell, I was ready to rope you and bring you home, if you had been having second thoughts about coming to the party."

"On your horse? That would have been interesting."

He laughed. "My pickup. Man, am I glad to see you. Everyone's given me such a hard time all week about chasing you off."

"I had a job to do." She sighed and told him about her flat tire. "I need to have it fixed before I return home. I wouldn't want to get a second flat and not have a spare."

"We'll take care of it."

"Thanks, Ted." She had hoped he would say they would and

that would be taken care of. Then she told him about Sims and his buddies.

Ted's face turned a little red and he frowned deeply at her. "Why didn't you call me?"

"I didn't want to ruin the party."

He grunted. "Your safety is more important to us than a party. Besides, we live to rescue damsels in distress."

She smiled.

"Seriously—"

"Seriously, nothing happened. They made me nervous when they followed me. They turned around when I drove down the road to the ranch."

"They followed you."

"Yeah, and I did think they might have had something to do with my flat tire, but maybe not."

"Except they just happened to have been following you for no reason, not heading in that direction, but following you."

"Right."

"So, it sounds suspicious to me since they turned around at the ranch road and didn't continue on their way."

"I didn't think they'd come out to the ranch, too many people with guns. But it would have been bad too, if they'd begun shooting up the place."

"I doubt they would have done that with all the people here. Their focus had been on going after the white cougar they'd shot the last time."

"I was thinking we might need to come up with a story about why my Jeep was parked where their truck was, beyond the Havertons fenced-off land on the old wagon road."

"We'll work on that too so we can all get our stories straight."

"Sims brought it up."

"What did you say?" Ted sounded worried.

"Nothing. I figured they would have told their lawyer what I said when I should have kept my mouth shut, which I did. No telling how a lawyer defending them could twist what I said."

"Right. Good thing you didn't say anything. Are you staying the weekend? You're already here and if they are waiting for you to return home, they'll have a long wait."

She smiled at Ted. "Oh, yes I'd love to see them sitting in wait, watching for my return, but I suspect they might think I'm staying for the weekend."

"I hope you're staying. We would have escorted you home tonight, though, if you had wanted to return there. I have half a mind to take your Jeep back to Grand Junction to see if they'll harass me while I'm driving it. And have Dan and some of his men as backup, of course."

"Yeah, well, I don't want to see any of you hurt for no good reason."

"They just need to learn you're not on your own and to quit trying to intimidate you."

"Well, I brought a bag just in case you asked me to stay. Besides, now I need to have my tire repaired and that will take a little time."

"Yeah, you know it. Everyone wants you to live permanently in Yuma Town so you can have more fun with a bunch of fun-loving cougars. Me especially. The ladies have a ladies' night out. We have barbecues, holiday celebrations. You would not believe all the stuff we do to celebrate being cougars here in Yuma Town."

"Larry Pierce hired me."

Ted smiled. "You gave notice at work already?"

"Uh, no. I'll do that on Monday. But where will I be staying once I move here?" She didn't want to presume that she would live at the bunkhouse with Ted when it was a ranch-hand house, not a place for permanent residents who didn't work out at the ranch.

"Here with me, if you don't feel it's too much of a commute for you. I wouldn't want it any other way."

She smiled, thinking that not only would she be with her hunky boyfriend nights too, she wouldn't even have to pay anything for housing right away. "I'm going to really like staying here with you just fine—as long as Kolby and the two new ranch hands are good with it."

"Yeah, they will be. They know that if the situation was reversed, I would be fine with it. And when Ricky was still living with us, Mandy and he hooked up and Kolby and I were both happy for them."

Still, she wanted to make sure because she knew Kolby wouldn't want to always feel he had to go off somewhere else to stay so she and Ted could have some alone time, not to mention the two new ranch hands either. They'd been staying somewhere else before they moved into the bunkhouse apparently.

CHAPTER 12

*S*tella was really excited about the prospect of working and living in Yuma Town. She couldn't believe how much her life had changed with that one little run as a cougar on private property. She had driven by the area numerous times before she'd finally made the decision to take the chance to run there. And it was the best thing she'd ever done. Of course, that was if she had a job here that she really loved. But everyone was so warm and welcoming before the party got started and she couldn't help but love it.

She needed to see Larry in person too, but Ted got an apple out of the fridge and took her to see Celestina in the barn first.

The horse immediately recognized Stella, her warm brown eyes focused on her. Stella stroked her nose, then fed her the apple and figured they would be friends for life. Stella was glad to see her again and couldn't wait to ride her.

After they left the stable, Stella saw all the women dressed in their western ballroom dresses, the guys decked out in their best western gear. And even Ted had put on a Stetson he only wore for social occasions. She had bought her first pair of cowgirl boots and thought these would be much better for riding horses in. Though not dressed in full, lacy petticoats. She couldn't imagine how woman could have ridden in those full skirts.

The kids were dressed in all kinds of costumes from pirates to vampires, to princesses and superheroes, black cats and even a mummy. Apparently, the western theme didn't appeal to them, but they were cute. The Haverton kids did wear a lot of western wear on a daily basis, so that was understandable. And the kids carried sacks for their goodies that they picked up from adults all over the place who were carrying candy with them to hand out, instead of doing a door-to-door affair.

The kids were running all over the place, but their parents, or others, were keeping track of them too. They didn't want to lose any of them during all the fun happenings.

She saw a Darth Vader in a helmet/mask, black clothes and a black cape and smiled. But because it was a western-themed event, at least for the adults, he was wearing black cowboy boots and a black and red bandana.

"That's Chuck Warner. He's in charge of the CSF in this region," Ted said.

"Too funny. I love how he added some western items to his wardrobe." She noticed when he walked and his black cloak billowed out, he not only had a lightsaber, but he also had a pistol at his hip. The kids all ran toward him to give him hugs. He was supposed to be the villain! At least in *Star Wars.*

"He's big into *Star Wars* and he loves the new *Mandalorian* series."

"With the baby Yoda? Me too!"

Ted smiled at her. "Then I'll have to watch them with you. I'm behind on the series."

Sacks containing battery-operated candles lighted the way to the haunted house and the corn maze. That was the good thing about their cougar eyesight though. They could see well as the sun set and it seemed like it was more beautiful all the time.

Though she suspected she noticed it more now that Ted was sharing them with her.

"The kids are adorable," she said. "I'm not surprised they didn't want to wear western clothes. They probably thought it wasn't Halloween enough."

"Yeah. Next year, they'll come up with something else. Who knows what though? But it's always fun to see what folks come up with. Some of the kids want to talk to you," Ted said.

She suspected they wanted to see her as a white cougar.

Stella was all set to dress in her beautiful blue gown, but it could wait as the Haverton kids assailed her first. "Are you really a white cougar?" "Can we see?" "Please?"

Then other children who had arrived came running over to beseech her to shift for them.

She smiled. Maybe she wasn't an oddity after all, but something special, especially in the eyes of the children here. And that made her feel really good. That's what she truly needed, besides Ted in her life—to feel like one of the gang and not like an oddity.

"Sure, I'll go inside the bunkhouse and change and come out to show everyone my white fur coat."

Ted was smiling at her.

She headed inside and then in Ted's master bedroom, she stripped off her clothes and shifted. As a cougar, she dashed through the bunkhouse, glad her arm and leg were no longer hurting—the first time she'd chanced being in her cougar coat since she was wounded and headed out the cougar door.

The kids cheered her as if she were a celebrity among fans. Everyone came over to take a look at her—adults and children alike. Some of the younger children stood back, as if they were afraid of the ghost cougar in their presence. What if she really wasn't a cougar shifter?

But the rest of the kids came over and petted her and gave her hugs, like she was a big pet cat that they loved. And for the first time since she'd been born, she felt loved and cherished and not like she was some aberration in the cougar shifter world. She was glad she had given them a show and tell, and even the little ones who were unsure at first as to whether to move closer to her, did, and petted her too. Maybe a little more tentatively than the older kids, but all she saw was the look of awe and genuine pleasure in all the kids' expressions, and in the adults' too.

When the parents started to say they needed to get on with the party and let Stella shift back so she could dress in her gown too, the kids reluctantly released their hold on her.

She raced back into the house and then she shifted in the master bedroom and put on her western ball gown, feeling genuinely like royalty. Once she had put up her hair and pulled on her western boots—blue and white to match her dress and that would go with her blue jeans, she left the bedroom to see all that Ted had in store for her tonight.

Ted was in the living room dressing the dogs in their Halloween costumes. He and the dogs were so much fun to be with. She laughed to see Koda and Zula wearing cowboy hats and bandanas tied at their necks. Zula's hat had blond braids attached which was the cutest thing ever. Stella took a picture of the dogs, both sitting for her and smiling eagerly, tongues hanging out, eyes on her—perfect little models and eager to please.

"They're a couple of photo hounds. Watch when we take them outside. They'll want to greet everyone, but then when people start taking pictures of them, they'll be professional models."

Stella laughed.

"Oh, and by the way. I told you everyone would think you were beautiful in your white coat of fur." He hugged and kissed her, and she did feel beautiful. Not just as a cougar, but dressed in her gown with a hot, sexy, male cougar hugging on her. "Both before and now. I'm one lucky guy. You would have had a dozen bachelor males interested in taking you to the party."

She smiled. "Yeah, but only you would have stood a chance at convincing me to go with you."

"I'm damn glad for that."

"Even though Larry hired me," Stella said, "I..."

"Wanted to wait to say yes and give notice on Monday."

She smiled up at Ted. "I wanted to wait to say yes until tonight because I had to make sure everyone was happy for me to become part of the community."

Ted kissed her. "Don't tell me you were concerned about being a white cougar and that some wouldn't like you being here."

"Sorry. It had crossed my mind."

"You have nothing to be sorry about. They all love you, if you didn't gather that from how everyone reacted to seeing you as a white cougar. You are precious to me and you're precious to our town. The kids adore you. I love you."

She smiled up at him. "Are you sure it's not too early—"

"No. I love you and I'm not taking it back."

She laughed. "I love you too." And she meant it with all her heart.

He kissed her and hugged her like he didn't want to let her go, but he finally said, "Then we'll celebrate that after the party. Do you want to get refreshments first or do the corn maze or the haunted house?"

"The haunted house."

He walked her outside with the dogs. "I have to warn you, it's not really scary. There are no chainsaws being revved up. For little kids, it's still scary, but not bad scary, just fun scary."

"My best kind of scary as long as you're there to protect me."

Ted pointed out Deputy Sheriff Stryker Hill and his mate, Deputy Sheriff Nina, at the Halloween party, both eating some food at one of the tables, dressed in western gear, but both were armed with guns. Stryker had two pistols and Nina had a side holster too, both of them wearing deputy sheriff stars on their chests. "They're here to have fun, but they are also here to serve and protect, just as though this were the old west. You might have noticed a few other men are armed. It looks like they're just wearing it for the period costume look, but because of the trouble we had, we don't want any surprises."

"That's why you're wearing a pistol at your hip."

"Yeah. For precaution. We want to be prepared if we encounter any specific hunters who want to cause more trouble. We doubt it, but just in case…"

"Good. I'm glad. I wish I could wear a gun and look as cool as Nina."

Ted smiled. "You look beautiful the way you are."

"I probably look like the school marm who would make more of a damsel in distress than someone who is exciting and fascinating."

"Do you know how to fire a gun?" Ted asked.

"Sure, but I could go with a pretend one." She saw the Haverton's boys with plastic side arms. "Like those."

"Next time we have a western-themed party, I'll be sure to get you one."

Then they walked into the haunted house in one of the large outbuildings, filled with stacks of hay that had been set up for displays and eerie lights and walkways throughout to showcase various spooky creations. Ghosts hung from the rafters, flowing above via the circulation of giant fans. A fluorescent skeleton greeted them, sitting in the entrance, an empty beer bottle in hand.

Giant black spiders highlighted with fluorescent lighting and brilliant orange eyes all aglow sat on one bale of hay.

A green-faced witch in a long black gown, the sleeves long and jagged, her hat—tall and pointy—sat atop one stack of hay and smiled wickedly as they passed by, saying, "I will get you, my pretties." She was a real actor and Stella wondered who she was.

Ted leaned over and whispered to Stella, "That's Elsie, one of your nurses."

"Oh, with all the green makeup and witch's warts I would never have guessed."

A wizard wearing a long, white beard, and a pointy hat, his long blue and gold starred robes looking majestic as he carried a staff featuring a hand-carved cougar on the top, smiled broadly at Stella. "Welcome to my world, pretty lass." Then he waved his staff at Ted, scowling and said, "Begone, you rogue. Leave the winsome lass to me."

Ted smiled. "None of your spells will tear the lady from my arms, you cantankerous old wizard, you." Once they passed him by, Ted said, "That's Mick Sorenson, a bachelor, his mother Mae lives in town and is known as the cat lady. Mick is in charge of the U.S. Fish and Wildlife Services branch that Tracey works for."

"Ahh, okay, so he really did want to chase you off with his wizardry spells."

"You bet. A rare white cougar? You could be his familiar."

She laughed. "This is so much fun."

They were about to pass by a stack of hay where the actor or the display wasn't present, but suddenly, a cougar wearing a cape leaped onto the top of the hay and snarled at them.

Stella fell back against Ted, trying to get away from the threat, her heart beating like crazy, and then she and Ted laughed.

"Hey, Ricky, good job," Ted said.

Ricky inclined his head.

Ted and Stella moved on then. "He's the youngest deputy we have in the sheriff's office and still a kid at heart. But with Mandy due to have twins, well, I was going to say he would have to grow up quickly, but I think he'll always be a kid at heart."

"That's fun and his kids will adore him for it," Stella said.

"I agree. I wish I'd had such a fun father when I was growing up. I think my grandfather was so stern with my dad that he thought that was the only way to raise his boys."

"Except that you and Bill were getting into trouble," she reminded him.

Ted smiled at her. "Yeah. We tried out bungie jumping, for one thing, before it was a thing to do."

Some people behind them screamed out when Ricky scared them, and Ted and Stella laughed.

Then they had to move into a narrow space where hot air blasted them in short spurts, soap bubbles floated in the air, and rat tails assaulted their ankles. She was glad she was wearing cowgirl boots, though the pretend rat tails were still an eerie feeling as they slapped her boots. A mist descended on them and she had the sudden funny feeling that she was going through a car wash—a haunted car wash where nothing was as it seemed. Then a hand reached out of the dark and grabbed at her arm and she screamed and then laughed. This was just too much fun.

Since she had already warned Ted with her scream that there was trouble ahead, he was better prepared.

She didn't think the haunted house would ever end, and she was glad because she was really enjoying it. This party was better than any party that she'd ever been to. When they finally left the house of cackling and laughter, of screams and spooky music, she was ready to partake of the food.

They had a whole array of food from eyeball tacos—black olives filled with sour cream on top of the tacos, and spider devil eggs, with black olives cut up on top to resemble the backs of spiders and their skinny legs. Pirate pasta even with zucchini strips in the form of an "x" to mark the spot of the treasure within. And mummy dogs, hot dogs wrapped in strips of dough, and mustard drops for eyes. An orange cake was topped with ghosts and dripping chocolate, RIP headstones and eyeballs. Eyeballs seemed to be the theme, as Stella filled her dinner plate with tacos and some pasta, and even a mummy dog. She'd saved room for all the fun foods, but she hadn't expected everything to be so perfectly Halloween themed.

She'd go back for the sweets afterward. A green cake featuring Frankenstein caught her eye. And Halloween cake pops covered in orange frosting and black spiders looked good enough to eat. One orange frosted cake featured a black cat and another a white skeleton. And mummy, ghost, and witch cookies were featured too on the long tables covered in orange tablecloths.

But to drink, she was sticking with bottled water. Even the bottles of water had special labels—hers a witch's brew; Ted's a warlock's tonic.

And when she and Ted sat down to eat alongside the Haverton's family, jack-o'-lanterns and flowers of purples and oranges decorated the orange cloth-covered tables.

After they ate their fill, Ted danced with her to several dances and what she loved about him was that even though she knew he didn't want any other bachelor males to dance with her, he graciously let them. Maybe he realized he'd totally won her over because of her fascination with all things country and western. Mainly she loved how he would always do special things for her, like the white roses, and even when she came to the party this time, he had placed white roses on the dining room table at the bunkhouse she'd noticed.

Ted danced nice and close to Stella as they waltzed their way around the dance stage they'd set up. This was like being in a movie, she thought, as the band played the music and she was swept up in that and breathing in the scent of the sexy cougar holding her hotly against his body, their hearts beating in rhythm, their feet in sync with each other and the music. She barely noticed the other dancers as if it were just her and Ted dancing their hearts out. She hadn't danced in years, and certainly not dressed like a western princess with the cougar of her dreams. Because that's what Ted was to her. The man, who in such a short time, had stolen her heart.

She tilted her head up and looked into his blue-eyed gaze and he seemed to know what she wanted, or maybe he just suspected, and he leaned down and kissed her, still to the beat of the dance, never missing a step.

She was in heaven, in a dream come true. And she couldn't believe how a run in a new place had led to this, as if the stars had suddenly aligned and she had been put in the right place at the right time, though when she had been shot and bitten by a rattlesnake, she'd believed otherwise at the time. Still, it had all turned out the way it was supposed to, she thought, and she kissed him back, loving the intimacy between them that made her ache to take this further.

"You are so hot," Ted told her, whispering in her ear, "and I don't want to give you up even for two weeks."

She smiled at him and moved her arms so they were resting around his neck. "It won't be for long."

"It will be forever."

"You'll be busy. I'll be busy."

"I won't ever be busy enough."

She laughed. But she was glad he felt that way about her. Just like she had felt that way about him. Even at work, all she could think of was not only about the cougar Halloween party, but seeing Ted again, worried that maybe the infatuation between them was because she'd been injured, and he'd come to her aid. But when she'd arrived at the ranch tonight, she knew it was a whole lot more than that. He couldn't get enough of being with her and she felt the same way about him.

They were doing line dances and then waltzing together again. She loved both because they were great exercise and great fun, but she loved dancing with Ted close. She'd never had a boyfriend who even liked to dance. So she was glad she'd taken classes in college to learn how to dance just so she could know what she was doing with Ted and not step all over his feet.

Once they finished dancing, he took her back to the table for refreshments.

"This is just wonderful." She looked around at all the lights that made the place sparkle with electricity—the pumpkins, the haunted house, the table full of creepy crawly stuff that everyone who participated touched while blindfolded and tried to guess what the stuff was.

They had Frankenstein cake and more bottled water and then she said, "The corn maze is the next thing I want to do."

"That sounds good to me," Ted said.

At the beginning of the maze, a sign stated: If you are looking for the wizard of Oz, come in, welcome, but watch out. Nothing is as it seems. Follow the yellow brick road.

"Let's go," Stella said and began their journey through the maze where steppingstones in gold occasionally could be seen on the path. They reached a dead end and had to choose—right or left?

"I have no idea," Ted said, and she suspected he had helped with the maze and knew just where things were, but she appreciated him for letting her lead the way on this new adventure.

She chose right and halfway down the path, they found a stuffed monkey wearing a hat, vest and wings. "The witch's minion," Stella said, with a worried tone of voice, playing along with the game.

They heard someone scream and then laugh and Stella wanted to go in the direction of the scream. That sounded interesting. Before they could run that way, one of the dogs came racing their way still wearing his cowboy hat, startling her and she laughed.

Koda greeted them and they petted him and then he ran off and Zula came chasing after him. They petted her and then she tore off after Koda. Stella and Ted continued on their way.

Then they reached the scarecrow and the cowardly lion, the lion sitting on a bench, the scarecrow standing behind him with his hand on the lion's shoulder.

"Okay, so we found some of the characters in *The Wizard of Oz*." She wondered if they would have any live actors in here also. That would be fun.

"Why don't you take a seat and I'll take a picture of you sitting on the cowardly lion's lap," Ted said.

She laughed. "Only if you do."

Then together, they sat on each of the lion's straw-stuffed legs and smiled to take a picture of the lion's face between theirs.

"Okay, now us kissing," Ted said.

If any other cougar had wanted to date her, Ted was making sure that they knew she was with him.

She puckered her lips and so did Ted, then he snapped the picture.

They heard someone else coming—Chase and Shannon—and Shannon said, "I get to do this." She took several pictures of them with her camera.

"We can return the favor," Stella said, then took pictures of Chase and Shannon.

"Where are the kids?" Ted asked.

"They're with Dottie and Jack for a few minutes. We wanted to get a picture with the lion—just the two of us," Shannon said.

Then they heard more voices, kids' voices and a whole bunch of little kids showed up, Dottie and Jack herding them all into the area. "Momma, Daddy," the Buchanan's twin girls said, then Shannon was taking pictures of Dottie and Jack and their family and Jack took pictures of the Buchanans while Ted and Stella slipped away.

"That was fun," Stella said, as she took Ted's hand and ran with him through the maze, getting lost, and then realizing they'd backtracked. "I smell our scent here."

He laughed and they began again, then finally found their way to where Dorothy, her dog, Toto, and the Tin Man were stationed next to a haystack. They sat down to take photos with Ted's phone and then they were on their way again. She loved it because they'd actually have some memories to share. Though she wanted to share them with her friends at work, she didn't want them thinking they should come here to the party next year and ask for an invitation.

Then a cougar jumped over the cornstalks and landed in their path, startling them as Stella threw her arms up in fright and planted her hands on her chest, her heart thumping wildly. She suspected that wasn't part of *The Wizard of Oz* experience! She laughed.

"Ricky," Ted said, sounding just as startled.

Then Ricky did another jump over into the next path and two kids screamed, then laughed.

"I bet he's lost," Ted said, smiling. "Ricky always adds a bit of fun to every adventure. I guess his stint at the haunted house is over."

"You didn't sign up for that?" Stella asked.

"Are you kidding? I'm on a date."

She was glad Ted felt that way with her because seeing everything at the party wouldn't have been the same without him.

When they found the wicked witch of the north, they laughed. Only her black boots and green and black striped stockings were showing under a big bale of hay. And the ruby slippers were sitting on top of the haystack. Stella had to hold them up to show she was Dorothy, and the ruby slippers were hers. After Ted took a picture of them, they finally found their way out of the maze and saw a woman hurrying after Ricky, the cougar, carrying his clothes.

"That's Ricky's wife, Mandy, and she's a nurse at the clinic, if you recall seeing her."

"I do and she's pregnant, so no jumping over the cornstalks looking for an easy way out of the maze for her if that's what had happened," Stella said.

Then Ricky and Mandy went into the ranch house and Stella figured he was shifting and getting dressed in there.

Sheriff Dan was standing nearby and said, "Mandy and Ricky got turned around in the maze, she was telling me. She told Ricky to shift and find a way out for them because she was getting hungry, but by the time he leaped out of the corn maze, she had already found the exit."

Stella and Ted laughed.

Then Dan tipped his Stetson and hurried off to join his deputy sheriff wife, Addie, and their kids.

"This has been so much fun, Ted. I've really had a ball," Stella said.

"I'm glad you're enjoying it. Just so you know, Kolby is staying with his brother and Mandy in town for the weekend. The other two ranch hands are staying up at the main house in one of the guest rooms."

Stella was glad that she and Ted would have the bunkhouse to themselves this weekend and was thankful to everyone who had made that possible.

"Are you ready for a hayride?" Ted asked her, offering to help her up onto the wagon.

"Yeah, I am." With her big flouncy skirt, she truly felt like a princess.

He climbed in after her, and with the wagon filled with party-goers, they took off for a long ride around a maze of haystacks and through the pumpkin patch filled with scarecrows.

"It must have taken forever to make all of the rest of those scarecrows," she said.

"Yeah, I even had the kids' help, but you know little ones. After a while, they were done with the newness and off to chase each other around the maze."

"You did all the rest by yourself?" She would have loved to have helped him with the others.

"Kolby, Addie, Dan, Shannon, and Chase came and helped. It's all fun. The preparations, the actual party, and taking down everything, we do it as a big cougar family."

"Well, I might not have helped to set this up, but I'll certainly help you to take things down."

"You don't have to, but any assistance will be appreciated. We'll have a big barbecue for everyone who helps. That's how we celebrate too. We make it fun."

She squeezed Ted's hand, thinking about the situation when

she was shot, even though she should have just been thoroughly enjoying the festivities and not been thinking about that, but she worried about it. "So what do we say about me parking my Jeep on the other side of the fence?"

"How about that you ran out of gas? They won't know any differently. We did have your Jeep towed. It was headed in the direction of the ranch."

"If I ran out of gas, someone could have brought a portable gas can out to the Jeep, especially if I was coming to visit you all. Not only that, but I wasn't just parked off the side of the road, but way in on the old wagon road."

"You were afraid if anyone saw your Jeep on the road, it would be vandalized. It had some mechanical problem? And we had to have it towed? You thought you could make it on the old wagon road to the ranch, GPS messed you up maybe?"

"Oh, yeah, mechanical issue. That could work. Why I drove it off the main road was because I thought there could be a shortcut to the ranch, a gate, and I could call you and have you come tow the Jeep. Then when I reached the fence, my cell phone had no reception, or it had died on me and I didn't have the charger with me, you know, just one of those days. And I had to climb over the fence and walk to the ranch. Then I thought you were in the barn, went in there, and before we could have my Jeep towed, the hunters were shooting at the barn, and I was hit."

"Sounds plausible, and we can practice the story. Really, you did a lot of that. Parked your Jeep at the fence, leaped over it, albeit as a cougar, and headed to the ranch, and hid in the barn. So except for a few human additions, that works."

"And the Jeep trouble?"

"Transmission issues. We'll have a mechanic in town verify he took care of your Jeep. And that's only if you have to say anything about that. They probably won't bring it up because obviously you weren't trespassing on the ranch land."

She smiled. "Not as a cougar."

"Right, and you were friends with us, so it wouldn't make sense that they'd mention it. But just in case, we'll have a story for them. Though I'm sure the prosecution will call the question irrelevant before you'd have to answer it."

"Okay, good, I'd rather not have to say anything about it at all."

"I agree. Even the smallest lies can get a person into trouble."

After the hayride, Larry Pierce came over to speak with them then, as if he thought it was the perfect opportunity. "I'm glad you're coming to work for me."

"I'm excited to get started and have the opportunity to work for you. I'll give my notice on Monday, and if you can wait for two weeks, I'll start working for you then," Stella said.

"You can't know how pleased I am to hear it. That certainly works for me."

She exchanged phone numbers with him, and Larry gave her a handshake and she shook his hand back.

"When Ted came to see me about updating his will, I asked him how you were feeling after what had happened out at the ranch. He told me you were fine and that you were a paralegal and that set the ball rolling for me to hire you right away."

Stella slipped her arm around Ted's waist and squeezed. "I'm glad Ted talked to you about it and you wanted to hire me."

"See you in a couple of weeks then. I'm off to see my sister." Then Larry headed across the grounds.

"That's Yvonne Mueller, Larry's sister, and she's a former FBI agent and now a bank loan officer in Yuma Town. Her husband is also a former FBI agent and the bank president."

"That's so cool." Stella sighed. "I can't thank you enough for everything everyone has done for me here."

"It's just part of who we are. We see a cougar in need, and we do everything we can to help out."

And keep them there too? Which for her, worked out perfectly.

CHAPTER 13

*L*ater that night after the Halloween activities ended, Ted and Stella ran with other cougars across the pastureland, and then when they returned, Ted and Stella said goodnight to everyone as families left with little ones and some of the mated couples still hung around visiting, but Stella was ready to call it a night with Ted. She'd been missing him and wanted to just chill out. Sure, tomorrow, she would help to clean up things, but she wanted to make love to Ted.

The two weeks she had left at work would go by quickly as she made plans to move, but still, she wished she'd already done it and she was here and staying and not returning.

She'd had so much fun and seeing Ted again made her realize that her thinking about him hadn't been just a euphoric delusion.

"I can't believe how much you've opened my world up to the cougar happenings, and how fun it has been," she said.

"I'm more than glad you're joining us for good. And me, especially."

* * *

Ted was thrilled that Stella was having such a delightful time with him at the Halloween festivities. He'd about knocked himself out trying to get everything ready, more than he had at any past event, wanting to thrill her and wanting her to come here to stay here. *With him.*

He couldn't thank Tracey enough for renovating the bunkhouse and making it a place that appealed to Stella too, enough so that she could stay there with him until they finalized other plans.

Once they were in his bedroom, that he was now seeing as *their* bedroom, he pulled off her cowgirl boots, glad she had picked them out for the dance, and they would be great for riding Celestina. He began to help Stella out of her long dress and smiled at the full slip she was wearing that had made her skirt have the fullness. Then she was all legs and bikini panties, not pantaloons like the ladies would have worn in the old days.

He pulled off her socks and then she helped him off with his boots. Then she was tackling his big buckle featuring a cougar, naturally, and once she'd unbuckled his belt, she slid his zipper down and he was so ready for her. Even dancing with her had turned him on, and he could have danced the night away with her.

She tugged his jeans down his hips, and he pulled them off the rest of the way. Socks were yanked off and tossed aside. Then he began kissing her again, his hands cupping her face, but she was still busy undressing him as if she couldn't wait to take this to the bed.

She was unbuttoning his vest and then pulling it off his shoulders and arms. Then she was working on the snaps on his western shirt, while he was kissing her again. He reached up and pulled her hair loose from the clip that was holding it on top of her head, letting the silky dark strands fall over her shoulders. He ran his fingers through the soft curls but had to relinquish the task when she started to unsnap the snaps on his long sleeves. First one, then the other.

Her bra was next to go, a pretty, blue lacy creation that hugged her breasts like he was about to do. Once he'd freed her of the lace, he placed his hands on her breasts and gently squeezed. She sighed against his mouth and he teased her tongue with his.

For a moment, they were caught up in the kiss, his hands on her buttocks, pulling her body closer and her hands on his face, as if she cherished him like he cherished her.

But then she slid her hands done his sides and reached for his waistband and pulled his boxer briefs down his legs until he could kick them aside. Then he was sliding her blue lace panties off her and ready to take this to the mattress. He lifted her up, her legs wrapping around him as he moved onto the bed. He was so eager to penetrate her slick sheath, but he needed to make sure she was just as ready for him as he was for her.

He began kissing her mouth again, loving her warmth and sweetness and softness. Loving her.

* * *

STELLA WAS SO ready to be Ted's one and only, just as she was ready for him to be her one true love. He was everything she had dreamed the perfect—well, not that everyone was perfect—but close to it—mate would be—with the added benefit? Her dream hero was a real cowboy. And man, did working on the ranch make him ripped in all the right places. She loved that about him, running her hands over his sculpted chest, feeling his biceps tightening as he swept his hand down her breast, her belly, and worked his way down to the area between her legs that was aching for his touch, his penetration.

He began to stroke her, tentatively at first, then firmer, faster while he watched her face, looking to see her response. She was lost in his touching her nub, the way he was working her, trying to bring her to pleasure, before he began kissing her again, as if satisfied he was doing it right. As if he was hitting the right erotic spot with enough vigor and determination to make sure he attended to her needs.

The intimacy between them escalated. She kissed him back more passionately, seeking and gaining entrance, stroking his tongue and pulling back, enticing him to do the same with her. And he obliged as if they already knew each other's every move. Their pheromones were all over the place, the musky smell of their sex encouraging them to take this further, to keep going, to not stop for anything.

As if he were stopping, or as if anyone would call on him to stop, she figured. This was their time and the way they conquered it would be the beginning of a beautiful relationship that had begun with pain and terror.

This was what she needed in her life. *Him.* A cougar who saw her as being beautiful, no matter what color fur she wore.

"I love you," he said against her mouth, his fingers still working the magic down below.

"I love you too." She felt like she was climbing to the top of the cliffs, eager to crest them. To feel the exhilaration of Ted's touch. To see the world in a different way. She was sliding her hands over his body, feeling the heat against her fingertips, the muscles rippling with effort. He was beautiful on the outside, just as much as he was on the inside.

His scruffy whiskers brushed against her cheek as he nuzzled her, and then he was kissing her again, his blue eyes like pools of deep water, heavily lidded, his every enhanced cougar sense taking everything in like hers were. His erection was pressing against her leg, steel rod and ready for action and she was ready for him. Wet. Hot. Eager.

Just a little bit more and she would reach the top of the cliffs. Just a little bit more and—she cried out, the orgasm hitting her before she was ready and she smiled at him and he kissed her mouth, moving his hand to her breast and cupping it.

"Are you ready?" he asked, in a husky, turned-on way.

"Yeah, always." And that earned her one of his sexy smiles.

He pushed her legs aside and began to penetrate her with the tip of his weeping penis, and then he was in all the way, and then thrusting hard.

Oh, yes, this was what she had dreamed of at night. Being with Ted in the throes of passion, but it wasn't anything like the real thing—of feeling his body sliding against hers and his stiff erection plunging deep inside her. Or his fingers stroking her to climax first.

She breathed in his manly scent, tasted the sweet treats he'd eaten at the party on his tongue and mouth, felt the heavenly way his hand swept down her side and then brushed away a curl on her cheek and he kissed her there. He didn't ease up on thrusting into her as if he couldn't stop himself if he tried, and she didn't want him to. And then he was slowing and thrusting hard as if he was near the end.

"Oh, Stella, yeah," he said, exploding deep inside her, groaning out the words, "you are mine."

She smiled at him and hugged him close. "I'm not giving you up for anything, yet, there are a bunch of women at work who would switch places with me in a heartbeat."

He finally moved off her and he draped his arm across her chest, smiling at her, looking as satiated as she imagined she looked. "They would never fill your shoes."

"No one would ever fill your cowboy boots either." And they snuggled for a long time, just enjoying the aftermath of their lovemaking.

She realized by making love to him, telling him she loved him, and his telling her he loved her, everything had changed between them. Now, she was truly eager to resign her job.

* * *

IT WAS FINALLY time to just sleep, to dream about the changes in Ted's life, the good changes that would last forever.

He was glad he'd found Stella to be his mate and that she'd felt the same way about him as he snuggled in bed with her for the rest of the night. He did think of all the chores the other guys would have to do without him while he was having a vacation of sorts with Stella, but this was important too and he wouldn't give this up for anything.

When he awoke in the morning, despite having felt her leg across his legs, or her arm across his chest, her head resting on his chest, as if she were afraid—like him—that the dream would end and they wouldn't be together, he realized she was here with him, perfectly happy like he was. He thought of getting up and starting their breakfast, the early riser that he was, but he couldn't move a muscle in that direction. He loved feeling her snuggling against him and didn't want to wake her. Usually, when he woke, he was out of bed in a flash, no two ways about it.

But with her, he had a damn good reason to stay in bed with her. Before he knew it, he had drifted off to sleep again, and this time when he woke, she was smiling at him.

He chuckled. "I woke earlier and thought to get us some breakfast. But skipped that notion to cuddle with you longer."

"And fell back to sleep."

"Yeah, which proved to me I needed to stay in bed with you longer anyway."

"I've been awake for a while and thought to get up and make us breakfast, but I know you don't sleep late in the mornings and no way was I going to wake you because of it."

He smiled and leaned over and kissed her forehead. "Why don't we get up and have breakfast and go for a ride then?"

"Oh, yeah, I'd like that." But we need to clean up the Halloween stuff."

"Yeah, but not until a little later. Everyone will be getting up in a bit after having such a late night." But then he got a call from Hal and hoped it wasn't work related.

"Hey, Ted, you know the offer still stands on the 150 acres. We have 800 acres. 650 is good enough for us. You carve out a section of land and build a house on it if you and Stella are heading in that direction," Hal said.

"Yeah, we are, and we're mated. We'd like a parcel of land down by the river, but high enough elevation that when we have floods, the house will be safe. You know the area I mean that I showed you before, if that's all right with you."

"Hell, yeah. You know in truth, having another home on the acreage will help to provide more eyes on the property. And more room at the bunkhouse for the two new hires we have."

"Thanks, Hal."

"Tracey and I wanted you to have it. Ever since you became part of our family, I've wanted to give you the acreage. Nothing's changed except you are mated and you need a homestead to call your own."

"Okay, well we sure appreciate it."

"Oh, and congratulations on the mating. I think you worked even faster at it than I did."

Ted laughed. "I thought you worked fast." Then they ended the call and Ted told Stella, "Hey, honey, we've got our own homestead."

"What?"

"One-hundred and fifty acres."

"Ohmigod, we're land rich." She hugged Ted tight.

He kissed her. "Yeah, we are. And we'll set the house on the property that overlooks this river, right here." He showed her a map of the property. "It's the area I had always wanted if I ever found a mate and finally took Hal and Tracey up on their offer of owning the property."

"We can fish in the river," she said.

"And paddle in it. And swim in it too, during hot summer days."

"When you took care of me in the barn, I had no idea it would mean me being mated, having a new job, a real home, and acreage. It's like a dream come true."

"You are that for me. We'll have to build some stables out there so we can have the horses whenever we want to ride. It also means we'll have to have security cameras up to serve as sentry duty, just in case any hunters show their faces out our way."

"But it's still safer than being in Grand Junction," she said. "Right?"

"You'd better believe it. We have each other and all of Yuma Town to protect us." He kissed her and she kissed him back. "We can ride out there and see the property."

"I can't wait to see it."

Once they had apple cider donuts and sausages, they took the appaloosas out for a ride across the valley. The sun had already risen but it was socked away behind building clouds and it looked like they were going to get some rain.

Both horses were eager to get out and exercise and Stella and Celestina were getting along famously. "Have you thought about a wedding date and where to have the ceremony?" He wanted to get the plans rolling.

"Here. I'm not sure about the wedding date. Uhm, maybe in between Thanksgiving and Christmas? That way we can see your family for Thanksgiving, and they can return here for Christmas and the wedding?"

"Okay, that sounds good to me." Tying the knot was something he didn't want to delay doing. "And we could go over house plans this weekend while you're here."

"Yeah, that would be good. For the wedding, even Koda and Zula should be there, freshly washed, smiles on their faces, tongues hanging out, him in a bowtie and her in a lacy collar. I'll never forget how both the dogs were sleeping by my side, as if protecting me while I was resting from my injuries."

"Yeah, I was looking for them and Kolby said they went into the bunkhouse. I couldn't believe I'd find them sleeping next to the guest room bed."

"You let them stay."

"Sure. They were worried about you."

"Thank you."

He didn't mean to get them all scheduled up with stuff, but he did want to iron out some things so they could begin building their own place and figure out the wedding plans. "I figure once you've moved into the bunkhouse, you can get with the other ladies and talk about the wedding. But for this weekend, I want you all to myself."

She laughed. "There will be time enough when I move here to work on wedding plans."

"Right. And the weekend in between, after you give your two-weeks' notice, we'll be busy packing up your place."

"And other stuff."

He smiled. "Yeah. The other stuff takes priority over anything else."

"And then I'll finish moving the next weekend and we'll be here."

But he was thinking, unless she had a lot to move, he wanted her here for that last weekend. He'd move her Friday night and then be here for the whole weekend so they could have fun together.

"You know, I should have thought of this before we said 'I do,' but what if our kids are white cougars too?"

"They may be, and they'll be adorable. The only difference is that you have a whole bunch of cougars to love them, and they won't be given up for adoption, or served emancipation papers. They'll be loved by everyone, whether they're white furred or tanned furred."

She sighed. "Okay, good. I thought about it once, and we've had so much going on, I forgot about it. But if you hadn't thought of it, I wanted to be sure you could back out of the relationship before we got married, if it bothered you too much."

Smiling at her, he shook his head as they walked the horses through the woods. "You're mine for keeps. I did think about our offspring, but only in passing and they will be much loved no matter what."

She breathed a sigh of relief again.

"I know you've suffered from this your whole life, but you really are just one of us now," Ted said. "Nobody wants to lose you for any reason. Your parents and your adoptive parents didn't know the treasure they had in their midst. We do. I do."

"That's why I love you. You say such nice things, but you mean them too. Did you want to run as cougars tonight to the waterfall? I want to check out the area behind the waterfall and climb the cliffs to see what's beyond them."

"Absolutely. It might be rainy tonight, but I'm game if you are."

"Maybe earlier then. It would be more fun if we're not getting soaked on the run there."

"Okay, we'll think of something else to do when it's raining."

She smiled at him. "A western movie."

"And more." He planned to do more when they got home from riding and after they had lunch. Or before. With Stella, he was always just winging it. He loved doing what she loved doing, so he was good with whatever they came up with.

Then they would help take down Halloween decorations afterward.

"Did you get the fixings for the steak fajitas? Ever since you mentioned them last weekend after I was injured, I've been craving them."

"I did indeed. Would you like them for lunch?"

"Yes! I will think of nothing else until we return home."

Then he steered them to an old stone building off in the distance.

"What's that?"

"The old homestead. The Havertons have owned this property for ages."

"Oh, if I'd known of this, I could have hidden here after I was shot."

"You never would have made it. It's too far from the main ranch house and we never would have found you in time."

He dismounted from Pablo and tied him to a tree branch, and then helped Stella down. Then he tied Celestina next to Pablo. "Okay, this is a rattlesnake haven, but we can have a peek inside. They'll overwinter in old buildings like this. But as cold as it is, if there are any in there, they'll be sluggish." He used his phone light inside and they moved slowly into the building that had only half a roof, most of the walls still standing.

He didn't hear any rattling, and he figured nothing would come out to strike at them, though he was being cautious just in case. "Sometimes the kids want to come in here when it's hot, to get in the shade, but we tell them it's not a good idea because of the rattlesnakes that want to get in the shade too."

"This is so cool. I can't imagine living here way back in the old days." Stella shivered.

"Are you okay?" He rubbed her back.

"Yeah, it just brings back memories of being bitten."

Ted should have thought about that. He took her riding all over, showing her the pastureland and forested land, the river and the site where he would have the house built.

"This is beautiful, Ted. Can we have a rock wall around a garden too?"

He smiled. "You bet. I've often come here to view the beauty of this spot, thinking the whole backside of the house would have big windows to look out on the mountains and the river. It's high enough that the house would never flood if the water rose, but we can just run out the back door and play in the river. With kids? It'll be perfect."

"This will be perfect. And we can see the sun setting in that direction and—"

Three deer ran across the property and stopped to drink way off in the distance at the river's edge.

"And see all the wildlife too. This is just beautiful."

"Yeah, but I would never have taken Hal and Tracey up on their offer of the land until I met you. And then, I knew it would be the place to build our own home."

She smiled at him. "Our first real home together, and our first real home."

"Yeah, it couldn't be more perfect." He was glad she loved the land as much as he did. He knew the whole lay of the land, or he would have asked her where she wanted to put a house. But she seemed thrilled, so he was glad.

They heard thunder off in the distance then, and Ted said, "Let's head on back before the thunderstorm catches up to us."

On the return to the bunkhouse, they spied more deer racing across the pastureland.

"I bet you have tons of wildlife here," Stella said.

"Yeah, goats, deer, bear, coyote, an occasional wolf, and lots and lots of cougars. Not to mention a wide variety of birds— several different kinds of waterfowl. It's a great place to teach the kids about the wildlife that lives in our area. We taught the kids how to swim in the lake, the ponds, how to climb the cliffs as cougars and—"

"How to ride horses," Stella said.

He smiled at her. "Yeah. I'm sure glad you love the horses."

"And everything western—one cowboy especially."

By the time they arrived at the stables, it was pouring rain and they put the horses up, rubbed them down, and fed them before they headed inside to shower and make lunch. He'd had a great time already with Stella, but he hated how fast the weekend would slip by and he'd be missing her all week long.

The Australian shepherds both ran up to greet them as they came in from the rain and Ted shook his head. "You two are a wet mess." Ted grabbed a couple of old towels and began drying Koda.

"Don't the dogs usually stay at the main house?" Stella grabbed the other towel and began drying Zula.

"Here with me usually. But Kolby's been taking them to get them out of our hair for the time being."

After making love in the shower—no plans were better than scheduling things out sometimes—they made the fajitas together. Usually when Ted and Kolby took turns cooking, one would cook, the other would clean. But Ted had fun actually making the meal with Stella. Though he hadn't expected her to hug and kiss him while he was cooking, when he was usually totally focused on the task at hand. And that made it even nicer.

They finally sat down to eat, and she raved about his fajitas and how they were the best she'd ever eaten.

She wasn't kidding and she placed an order for more. He laughed and obliged. They'd worked up an appetite since breakfast.

The rain was beating down on the roof and the lightning was streaking across the sky in sheets and then forking to the ground, thunderous booms sounding minutes later.

"I guess none of us will be helping to take stuff down from the Halloween party for a while," she said.

"No. It'll get done eventually. Do you want to watch a movie?" he asked, after they ate the rest of their fajitas and then cleaned up the kitchen.

"Yeah, anything you want. It doesn't have to be western, really. I love everything."

So they picked a futuristic dystopian story, he started a nice fire in the fireplace to warm them up and they snuggled under a plaid blanket on the couch, the rain pouring in waves, the wind blowing, the lightning flashing across the sky, and the thunder booming overhead. He just hoped they wouldn't lose their electricity, though he knew what he was doing if they did. Forget flashlights and lanterns. He was taking Stella back to bed.

They ended up watching another movie after that, the storm not letting up and he made mulled wine to drink while they enjoyed the movie. This was nice, being with Stella like this. It wasn't the same as watching movies with Kolby, though luckily, they liked the same kind of stories, but snuggling with Stella was super nice.

When it was time for dinner, Stella wanted more fajitas.

Ted laughed. "Sure, I've got more." He had enough to make them for Kolby and the other ranch hands too, and extras in case they wanted them. His mother had always told him it was better to have more than enough food for a meal, than not enough—when she was entertaining guests. And since Kolby was at his brother's house for the weekend, and the other ranch hands at the main house, Ted had plenty of fixings for more fajitas for Stella and him.

"Good," she said, and she was already cutting up more bell peppers, really getting into the role of being his assistant chef. Or maybe learning how to do this if he wasn't around and she wanted to fix these for herself. Like even next week while she was still at the apartment in Grand Junction.

"I'm glad you're enjoying them."

"Oh, I am. I've only had them this good on a trip once. They were out of this world, but you managed to top even those."

CHAPTER 14

$\mathcal{A}$fter dinner, Stella and Ted worked on a board game and when the sky cleared, Ted called the Havertons to see about taking down Halloween decorations and got a hold of Hal.

"We took down the dance stage and pulled up the dance floor. Some of the fall stuff is being left up for Thanksgiving, including the scarecrows. We already put away the Wizard of Oz characters before it rained. There wasn't really that much stuff to put away in the haunted house, so it's done. We're good, so don't worry about it. You can help with the scarecrows after you return from Thanksgiving, if they're still up by the time you return from Texas."

"Are you sure?"

"Yeah, Ted. Hell, you work all the time. You and Stella just have a good time."

"Thanks," Ted said, and he was glad for it. When they ended the call, he said, "Okay, no working on the Halloween decorations. It's taken care of."

"Oh, okay." Stella wanted to run as a cougar. Ted was always game, and the two of them stripped, then shifted and ran out the

150

cougar door without another moment's hesitation. With the clouds slipping away, they would be able to see the sunset and he was glad for that since they hadn't been able to enjoy one at the falls yet.

He had to remind himself that they had all the time in the world now to enjoy the sunsets once she moved here and that made him feel really great.

They raced across the pastureland and through the woods, then finally made it to the pond. It was sparkling in the shining sunlight that had just begun to set. For a moment, she stood watching it, then she licked his face, and tore up the cliff face.

He took off after her, having the time of his life. They finally leaped on top of the boulders until they came to the peak of the cliffs and sat there together, watching the sun set.

It was beautiful up here, especially sitting with his mate, who was the most riveting color of all.

They watched geese flying overhead toward a lake and saw a bear rambling off in the distance through a meadow to a stream. Both of them watched the black bear, instantly captivated. At least the bear was on the other side of the ridge, the waterfall and pond behind them. Though if it was one of the bears he'd met this summer, who was a shifter, they had nothing to worry about. The sun continued to sink in the sky, coloring the drifting clouds pink and gold and red. Then he saw a rainbow cross the sky and he licked her face. She licked his back, acknowledging she had seen the majesty of the rainbow too.

When the sun was nearly gone, she bounded back down the rocks, the chilly breeze whirling around them as they made their way down to the bottom. With night vision cat eyes, she could see in the fading light as she swam across the pond to the waterfall and beyond. Their cougar coats kept them warm and he swam after her and found her looking through the screen of water at him.

He moved through the spray of the waterfall and joined her, winding around her, rubbing against her body like cats do and licked her face.

It was time to return to the bunkhouse, shift, take a hot shower, and more loving.

* * *

THE NEXT MORNING, Ted and Stella were making breakfast—cinnamon pancakes, and pumpkin spice lattes, and she had the notion to return to the cliffs where she'd been shot so that she would have no fear of the area. "Have you found the spent shells around the cliffs where I was shot? At least the blood would have been washed away during yesterday's storm."

"We had rain while you were sleeping in the clinic too. Dan told me that there was no evidence of blood anywhere that you had left behind, and we cleaned up the hayloft and the barn where the rain couldn't wash it away, so you're good there." Ted got on his phone and then put it on speakerphone. "Hey, Dan, Stella was asking if any evidence was left behind where the hunters had shot her on the cliffs, or near there."

"We cleaned them up, and then we took pictures of the shots fired at the barn and the casings left all over the place. We have several rounds we dug out of the barn walls. All of it was taken into evidence, including the two that Vanessa dug out of Stella's arm."

"Okay, good."

"As cougars, we can still smell where the shooting took place earlier, and we can smell the blood, but the evidence of the blood is at least washed away, so if the men try to have a lawyer attest to the fact that they shot a cougar and the trail of blood led all the way to the barn, it won't fly."

"That's good news." Ted asked Stella, "Did you want to ask the sheriff anything else about the shootings?"

"No, that sounds like we're covered, story-wise," Stella said.

"Thanks, Dan, we're about to eat breakfast. I'll check in with you later," Ted said.

"Have a great day." Dan ended the call.

Ted and Stella ate their pancakes.

"I want to go out there," Stella said.

Ted frowned at her. "To relive the trauma?"

She sighed. "No. I just want to prove to myself the hunters are gone and not out there looking to shoot a white cougar."

"We can ride out there."

"You don't want me to go in my white fur coat."

"No. I can't help but worry that they got the word out to someone about the injured white cougar. So unless we run at night or in the morning before daybreak or just farther away from where they claim to have shot you, I don't want anyone to see you as a cougar running in that area."

"Okay. We can ride there. I would love that. And I'd probably feel safer anyway." Though she had wanted to climb up on the rocks as a cougar, to prove to herself that she was really safe there and that the men wouldn't be there to shoot her again. "What about the rattlesnake?"

"It's too cold for them to be out and about. We had that one day where the temperature had risen, but not now."

"Should we take the dogs?"

"Not this time. They need to help Kolby and the other ranch hands with the cattle. The new guys need to learn how to give the dogs commands too, and the dogs need to learn to obey them."

"Okay."

After cleaning up from breakfast, they headed out on the appaloosas to ride. Ted was amazed how much Stella loved riding horses, like she'd been born to it when she'd never been around them much.

"I was dying to ride when I was younger, but my adoptive parents were afraid of how the horses would react to us and rear up and injure us, because we smell like cougars. When I was emancipated, I did my one and only trail ride. I loved it, except that the horse kept trying to knock me off his back, and the trail wasn't that interesting. I love how we can go anywhere all over the acreage," Stella said.

"Yeah, and the seasons make it appear different too, so even if you're going to some of the same areas, you'll find flowers or snow or fall colors that make it appear completely different." He hoped Stella was feeling all right as she followed the direct path that she had traveled as a wounded cougar. It even made him feel stressed out, but if she needed to do this for her own peace of mind, they had to do it. He didn't want to ask if she was feeling all right either, if she just had to live in the moment. Instead, he talked to her about other things that were more cheerful, he hoped.

He told her about how Ricky had been turned and how he had turned his brother, and they'd chased each all over the clinic as cougars when they had been recovering from their injuries. "They created all kinds of havoc."

Stella laughed. "I hadn't realized they were more newly turned."

"Yeah, and Ricky turned Mandy by accident. He turned his brother on purpose though. The brothers were close to each other and Kolby had practically raised Ricky, so Ricky couldn't imagine being here among cougars—and we wouldn't let him go because he'd been newly turned—without his brother being a part of the community."

"And Mandy?"

"Oh, she was Ricky's ex-girlfriend."

Smiling, Stella raised a brow.

"Mandy ran into him with her car." Then Ted told the rest of the story and Stella laughed.

"Being a cougar has always been kind of a negative thing in

my book, so I'm glad that I can hear how being turned can turn out fine, and being what I am, can too."

"Yeah, we have to make do with what we have to work with, but we do that by celebrating what we are, and with so many of us here, we can do that in grand style."

"I'll say."

They finally reached the cliffs and she said, "I didn't realize it was as far as it was to the ranch. I thought it was just because I was trying to keep really low and I wasn't sprinting for safety like I wanted to do."

"It is a long way from the ranch. Those hunters had to travel a long distance to reach it."

"What if they start posting all over the social media sites that they injured a white cougar?"

"We've got more patrols out in this area, checking to make sure we don't have any hunters about. We would have done it for anyone if any of our cougars had been shot."

"Oh, good." Stella sounded vastly relieved.

"Yeah, we don't take chances when we have issues like this. If someone else had been hit, we could have the same situation— hunters or thrill-seekers searching for the wounded cougar. Even some good Samaritans who might want to rescue it could be searching all over the property. But with the notion we might have a rare white cougar, we could have a lot of different folks coming to check it out for various reasons."

They came around the cliffs and saw a sheriff department's vehicle parked in the area where Stella had parked her Jeep. Chase was up on the rocks and they looked up to see him waving down at them. "Good day for a climb."

"I want to join him." Stella climbed off her horse. Then she tied her up to a tree branch and Ted did the same with his horse.

It was much easier climbing the cliffs as a cougar, but no one was to go anywhere near here as a cougar right now, just in case hunters figured the cougar, or others, might have marked this as their territory.

They finally made it up to the top and stood there, looking at the majestic surroundings, seeing the horse ranch way off in the distance, but if he hadn't known what they were, he would have had to guess that the horses standing in the pasture were just that. So Stella wouldn't have known it before she raced for the safety of the barn.

"It's beautiful out here. Too bad hunters trespassing on the ranch lands had to spoil it for the rest of us, at least for a while," Chase said.

"I agree," Ted said, "but it's good to take note that we can't let our guard down when it comes to the cougars and other wildlife's safety."

"Right," Stella said. "It's too beautiful and the land needs to be preserved." Then she frowned at Chase. "Has anyone ever tried to grow illegal crops on the property since the Havertons have so much acreage?"

"Yeah, a couple of times. They were thinking the land was untamed, owned, but no one would be the wiser. But with our sense of smell, we can sniff out the illegal plants or stills and take them down quicker than they can put them up or grow their plants. We've caught the marijuana plants in the early stages of growth. The ones who were attempting to grow on the land found it wasn't profitable as much as we were watching for them. Not only that, but we arrested several of the men who came back to check on their plants, and even caught some planting one time. Thankfully, we have an army of law enforcement officials who can take them down."

"Even with legalizing pot in Colorado, they still plant illegally?"

"Yep. It has to do with the 'free' land to grow on and avoiding regulations and taxation. We haven't had any issues in the last couple of years, though we check out the acreage and others like it that the cougars own regularly," Chase said.

Which was another good reason to have his and Stella's home built in another area of the land—to help show there were too many eyes on the property for other illegal activities to take place, Ted thought.

CHAPTER 15

*S*tella was so glad to see Chase out checking the area for illegal hunters or for anyone else who might be "sight-seeing" for cougars.

And she was grateful to Ted for not trying to talk her out of coming here to see where she'd been shot and just, she didn't know, get it out of her system, she supposed.

She gave Ted a hug and thanked Chase and the others who were trying to keep the cougars safe.

"You're doing it also, just by being here, by riding the range with Ted, keeping a look out to see who all might be trespassing. With a presence in the area, it makes it harder for these varmints to be sneaky as far as illegal activities go," Chase said.

Then they said their goodbyes and Stella and Ted made their way down to the bottom of the cliffs. She slipped a couple of times, but Ted was right there to catch her, which she so appreciated. "I'm not used to wearing cowgirl boots to climb in."

"Yeah, cougar paws work the best, or hiking boots, but when you wear the cowboy boots as much as I do, it becomes second nature, and you can accommodate for any terrain." He helped her up on her horse. Then they rode off, but she waved back at Chase who was looking the area over using binoculars and he waved goodbye to them also.

"I feel better coming out to see this. Thanks for taking me."

"You're welcome. I wasn't sure if I could do that if I'd been shot there so recently, but I'm glad you feel better about it after seeing it could be safe," Ted said.

"I think seeing Chase up there helped and knowing that a lot of people, even me, in fact, are helping to keep it safe. That makes me feel good too. I think being a victim is awful unless you can take a stand and fight back. So in a peaceful way, it's a way to take action and stop the bad stuff from happening in the first place."

"I couldn't agree with you more."

Chase called out, "Hey, wait!"

"Did you spot any trouble out here?" Ted asked Chase.

"I thought I saw someone on the property off in that direction. I didn't see any vehicles parked along the road though—"

"I'll go check it out," Ted said.

"I could go with you," Chase said. "Stella can stay here to keep an eye out."

"I'd like to go with you," Stella said.

"If they're more hunters and they're afraid of getting locked up like the other guys?" Ted asked. "I don't want to risk you getting shot again."

"All right. Just be careful."

Ted knew Stella wanted to go with him, but he truly was worried about finding more hunters.

Chase and Ted mounted the horses down below, while Stella climbed up to the top of the cliffs with the pair of binoculars. He figured she would be perfectly safe while he and Chase confronted trespassers, if there were any.

They headed out across the pastureland, taking deep breaths of the air, trying to smell any scents of human activity in the area, watching for any sign of movement. They'd ridden for maybe a mile when he and Chase saw two men scramble into the woods, seeking cover beyond a creek.

He and Chase headed across the creek to apprehend the trespassers. Both had rifles, but the scent they left behind didn't smell like the other hunters' scents.

"Not them," Chase said.

"Nope. I'm hoping they're not here because of the others though."

They rode through the woods, following the scents of the men—scared, tense, sweaty from the long hike from wherever they'd come from. If Chase hadn't found any vehicle nearby, Ted wondered if the men had been dropped off to hunt, thinking no one would be the wiser.

They could hear them up ahead, crashing through the underbrush, breaking twigs in their path, typical of men fleeing from danger, not realizing the cougars could hear them now, even though they weren't really close yet. Then they saw one of the men duck behind a rock, while the other continued to run. A ploy?

Or it was an ambush? Ted veered off to ride behind the boulders while Chase headed around to the other side, the two of them in sync as far as pinning the hunter down. They'd catch up with the other hunter as soon as they handcuffed this guy.

As soon as they had both skirted around the boulders, they found the man had run off, yet they discovered where he had been lying in wait. He would have heard the two appaloosas' footfalls coming around either side of the boulders and must have made the decision to hightail it out of there. Ted was thinking that the hunter had thought they would continue to chase after his buddy, and wouldn't look for him behind the boulder, but the hunters didn't know the cougars' keen sense of smell had been his downfall.

They saw the hunter in question duck around some more boulders and Chase and Ted galloped after him. Chase called out,

"I'm Deputy Sheriff Chase Buchanan! Come out with your hands up or we'll be forced to take more extreme measures!"

The guy didn't move. Or maybe he was trying to crawl around the rocks and out of there. The only reason Chase had called out a warning to the hunter was because they couldn't take the horses where the hunter had gone. Smart move on his part.

Suddenly, a bear roared.

Holy hell! If it was one of the bear shifters they had encountered this summer, the bear could be at real risk. A hunter wouldn't hesitate to shoot it, saying his life was endangered, even if he was trespassing on private property and illegally hunting.

"If you shoot the bear, we shoot you," Chase called out, neither of them able to see the bear, but they were both off their horses, tying them to a tree, and rushing up the boulders as fast as humanly possible.

It was times like these that Ted wished he were a cougar about now.

He crested the top of the rock and saw the big black bear watching the hunter and recognized him at once as being the bear that went by the name of Blue.

The bear shifters were welcome on the ranch as bears or otherwise, hopefully free from being shot by hunters, but in this case, he was liable to be killed.

"Put your rifle down, right this minute," Ted shouted to the man. "He's a pet bear. You kill him, we'll have you up on so many charges, you'll never get out of jail." Not that they could charge the hunter with that much, but he had to make him believe they could.

The hunter looked terrified, and he definitely didn't want to put down the rifle.

"Blue, go, thanks for catching the hunter for us. Go eat some berries."

The bear grunted and headed off toward the waterfall.

"Now put down the damn rifle," Chase said, flashing his

badge. "Unless you aim to resist arrest or shoot an officer. I'm sure having attempted murder on your record won't help you much. And going to prison? Well, you might even miss the wife."

Ted noticed the man was wearing a gold wedding band then.

"What's your name and your friend's name and how come you are here, trespassing on private property?" Chase was still waiting for the hunter to comply. "Don't tell us you didn't see the signs or climb barbed-wire fence to trespass either."

He finally gave his name. "I was alone."

"We'll find the other hunter, rest assured," Ted said, but the guy wasn't putting his rifle down. Ted had had enough. He didn't want to leave Stella on her own for too long. He pulled off the rope he had strapped to his saddle and lassoed the guy, surprising the hell out of him and he screamed out.

The hunter dropped his rifle and Ted noticed then that the bear had turned to watch the situation just in case he was needed. But they didn't need him to help out, and Ted hoped that the hunter wouldn't tell the world that a pet bear lived on the ranch!

Still, Ted had had to say something that would protect the bear.

Chase handcuffed the man. "We should leave him behind and track the other hunter who had been with him. Great job with the lasso, Ted."

"I never thought I'd have to use it on a hunter."

"No, no, you can't leave me. What if the white cougar comes for me? Or the bear? He doesn't like me, only you. I wouldn't have any way to protect myself," the hunter said.

"Like they have no way to protect themselves when you illegally hunt them on private property?" Ted asked.

"You can't leave me here," the man insisted. "If they killed me, it would be on your head."

Ted and Chase only smiled at that.

"You can't!"

Chase and Ted reluctantly helped him get down from the

boulders. Ted shouldered the man's rifle and his own. Ted still wished they could have left the hunter behind and returned for him. Maybe he'd think twice about trespassing here then.

"You weren't so scared before when you were eager to kill on the ranch land," Ted said as Chase mounted Celestina, and Ted helped the man onto the horse. Then Ted mounted Pablo and they headed out at a gallop to track the other hunter through the woods.

"How did you learn about the white cougar?" Ted asked. Their own local newspaper hadn't reported on it, and he hadn't heard that anyone else had seen anything on it. Which made him suspect Sims and his buddies had mentioned it to these two men. "We'll find out sooner or later. We might even be able to connect you with Sims and his buddies who shot a woman at the ranch."

Chase nodded. "Yeah." He gave the man his Miranda rights because they had to do what was right as far as following the laws and due process and all that.

"I have a baby due in three weeks," the man sullenly said.

"And that has what to do with anything?" Chase asked. "You want to be there for the delivery instead of sitting inside a jail cell? You should have thought of that beforehand."

"Hell, man, a kid costs a lot of money."

"I have twins, tell me about it," Chase said. "It still doesn't tell us why you're illegally trespassing and hunting and risking getting yourself shot on private property."

The man left out his breath. "I know Sims, okay? He said if my friend and I could find the white cougar and take pictures of it—"

"With hunting rifles," Ted said.

"Well, hell, Sims said they shot it. So yeah, we had to bring hunting rifles in case we ran into a wounded cougar. Look at the bear that nearly attacked me."

"Pet bear, and he has been in several movies," Chase said. "I can't imagine you would want to tell the media how you had killed a beloved bear that was a film star."

Ted wanted to laugh. "Just think if your baby son or daughter—"

"Son," the hunter volunteered.

"Son," Ted continued, "learned someday that you killed the bear featured in their favorite movie."

Though Ted suspected the hunter would teach his son to hunt someday and a bear was a bear, wild and free to shoot.

"If I tell you what I know, will I get off easier?" the hunter asked.

"It depends on what you know," Chase said.

"Sims paid Fenton and me to kill the cougar, if it was still alive, to put it out of its misery. You know. A good deed. No hunter ever wants to make an animal suffer. He sent us after he told us what had happened. He said they tracked the blood all the way to the ranch so they know they hit it. And they knew it had to have been at the ranch."

"And they shot up the ranch, the barn, without going inside to find the supposed cougar?" Chase snorted. "How many years have you been hunting, man?"

"Thirty, since I was fifteen."

"And how many times have you heard of a white cougar?" Chase asked.

"Never. But we looked it up and there had been a trail-camera sighting of a rare young male in Brazil."

"And how far is that from here?" Chase asked.

"I'm not saying it's the same one, but that it's possible for them to exist."

They got quiet then and Chase and Ted smelled where the other man had run. They walked the horses through the woods, listening to the twittering of a couple of cardinals, male and female, and heard something rustling around in the underbrush —a rabbit, that took off lickety-split.

The other man's scent stopped, turned, and they headed in another direction.

They continued to walk the horses in silence, listening, taking deep breaths, watching for any signs of the other hunter. Ted suspected he would head for the main road and call for a pick up, but he was headed in the wrong direction. Had he believed they would head there too and arrest him? Or had the darn fool gotten himself lost?

Then they heard a rifle cock. What the hell did the hunter think he was going to do? Shoot them and free his friend?

"Don't shoot!" the hunter riding with Chase said. "Fenton, it's not worth it! These guys are deputy sheriffs!"

Not that Ted was, but if the hunter had inferred it, that worked for him. He was glad they hadn't taken the dogs with them this time, or the dogs would have chased after the hunters and could have been shot, though in retrospect, he could have left them with Stella so she would have had some protection.

"Give it up," Chase said. "You don't want to make things worse for yourself!"

CHAPTER 16

*S*tella wished she'd gone with the men, though she knew they'd only worried about her safety, but sitting on the rocks was boring. She was ready to walk home to the ranch and the bunkhouse so she could do something else, even watch a movie or something.

She pulled out her phone and realized she didn't have any cell reception. Great. If she ran into trouble, she couldn't call anyone. She hadn't realized that before when she was out here because she'd been running as a cougar.

She took a couple of pictures of the mountains, but with a cell phone, they weren't as great as if she'd had a camera with her.

Then she saw a black bear headed her way. Holy crap! Now what was she supposed to do? She didn't have a gun or rifle, not that she wanted to shoot the bear, but she would have fired a warning shot and chased it off, hopefully. She moved up higher on the rocks. He could climb up there, she figured. She was a sitting duck. He was sniffing the air, probably wondering if she would make for a good meal, though she didn't think humans were normally on the menu. And the bear didn't have cubs with him, or her, whatever it was.

He stood on his hind legs and though she was still much higher than him, it made chills run down her spine. Then he smelled the air and right before her eyes, he shifted!

Her jaw dropped. "Ohmigod, you're a shifter." Obviously. And big and naked and *big*. She really shouldn't be staring since she was used to some cougars stripping and then shifting around her. But not bears. Never a bear. That was big. Really big. She felt her face flush with heat.

"Ted and Chase captured one of the men and are after the other," the bear told her. "My name is Blue, and I'm a friend of theirs."

"Oh, uh, thanks for telling me." She motioned with her cell phone. "No reception way out here. I had no idea how things were going with them."

"Hopefully, fine."

Then shots rang out and he shifted in a blur of human and fur combined until he was a bear again and ran off toward where the gun shots rang out in the woods. "Ohmigod, no!" When Stella heard the shooting, she was glad she and Ted had left Zula and Koda at home. She knew they would want to go protect Ted and could have been shot. Her heart was beating like crazy and she wanted more than anything to help out, but she didn't have a gun and she knew she'd just put everyone else at risk.

She was afraid Ted and Chase had found the other hunter and he wasn't turning himself in. But the bear would be in peril if he got involved. She needed to get help to them, if they hadn't called this in themselves, but they might not have been able to if they couldn't get reception either.

She stared in the direction of the shots fired. Several more shots rang out. She felt a cold sweat cover her skin and she prayed Ted and Chase were okay. That if there were any casualties, it would be the man shooting at them.

Then she heard a vehicle pull off onto the old wagon road, and she was thinking help was on its way.

She held the binoculars up and searched the area for any sign of who was in the vehicle.

"Someone else is here," Sims said.

No! Sims was back? Was he friends with the two men Ted and Chase had been after? She wouldn't be surprised. Now she wished she had been armed. She could just envision being shot again—only this time as a human, for real, and she wouldn't live to tell the tale. When Sims showed up, she was again glad the dogs hadn't been with her. They would have barked and given their location away and she could just imagine the hunters shooting to kill them and both she and the dogs would have been in danger. She really didn't want to have to face that again.

"He told us to pick him up here," Clayton said. "Where the hell is he?"

There had been no more shots fired after Sims and his buddies had arrived. She could see all three men now from where she peered through the rocks, a gap between a boulder and two others that made for the perfect spy hole so she could stay low and hidden. The men didn't know that there had been a shootout. But who had won the confrontation?

She ground her teeth, wishing she could call someone, anyone, to come and arrest these men again. Though unless they climbed the fence, they weren't trespassing.

"Maybe we should climb the fence and see if we can locate them," Clayton said. "Hell, I don't have any phone reception."

"We could climb up on top of the boulders and see if we can get cell reception up there," Sims said.

No! No reception up here!

She looked around for some other location to hide herself. They probably wouldn't just shoot her, but what if they did? Still, just because they illegally hunted wild animals, rare wild animals, didn't mean they would shoot people. At least not on purpose.

She did have the notion that the men might leave if she stood up on the rock and told them she had just called the sheriff's department. But what if they shot her? Again?

Clayton held the barbed wire fence down with his boot and Sims crossed over the fence. They had crossed the line. Or at least Sims had. Now he was trespassing again. And he could be charged with it and maybe even returned to jail. She checked her phone. Still no bars.

Then the other man, Braxton, said, "I'm staying here with the vehicle in case Fenton and his friend show up." But he held down the fence for Clayton.

Clayton climbed over it and Stella was thinking the Havertons needed to put up a better fence to keep hunters off the land. She was still shocked about the bear, but glad he had run off and these men hadn't seen him. They were all carrying rifles. She'd thought they'd had them confiscated because of shooting her, but she suspected they had even more from where those had come from.

Then she saw a couple of Land Rovers tearing across the terrain toward the trees as Clayton started to climb up the cliff.

"Hell, that doesn't look good," Sims said. "Let's get out of here."

"You think someone caught them trespassing?" Braxton asked.

"Maybe. Hopefully they shot the cougar before we arrived and they already sent us pictures of it," Sims said.

"Well, if they didn't, they don't get paid for the job," Clayton said.

"You know," Braxton said, getting his keys out. "If they got caught, they could spill the beans on us."

Sims scoffed. "They wouldn't dare."

Then Clayton pushed the barbed wire down so Sims could get over the fence, and then Sims reciprocated while Braxton had hurried to get into the truck and started the engine.

"We better hurry," Sims said. "Looks like one of those Land Rovers is on its way to the cliffs."

"Hell, do you think they saw us?" Braxton asked.

"We'll be out of here before they reach us and they'll never know we were here," Sim's said, climbing into the passenger's seat up front.

"What about the cougar?" Clayton asked, moving faster now as he jerked the truck door to the back seat open and jumped in.

"We'll have to come back some other time. I'm determined to prove we were right," Sims said.

Clayton slammed the back door shut and Braxton drove off down the old wagon road.

Stella breathed a sigh of relief that they were gone, but she was so worried about the others, she could barely think straight. She saw Hal driving the Land Rover toward her as she used the binoculars to make him out.

She was glad someone was coming for her, but she sure hoped everyone else was all right. She waved from her perch above and then headed down the cliffs, carefully. She didn't need to fall and injure herself.

Then she was down at the bottom just as Hal pulled the Land Rover to a stop.

"What happened? Is everyone all right?" She hurried to get into the vehicle. She wanted to tell Hal about Sims and the others, but she had to know about Ted and Chase.

"Ted and Chase are okay. They had to shoot Fenton, one of the two hunters. The other had gone with Chase and Ted. He was handcuffed. But Fenton was shooting at them, not about to be taken into custody."

"Don't tell me. He has warrants out already for his arrest."

"Yeah, he does. The other man doesn't. A couple of traffic violations is all. But the guy he'd come out with? Fenton? He murdered a family in Denver, and he'll be sent up there to face charges. He has been shot, not fatally, but Ted shot him in the arm and Fenton might have lost the ability to use that arm."

"But the guys are all right?"

"Yeah, the hunter with Fenton? Man, was he mad. Fenton

could have killed him in the barrage of bullets Fenton was firing at the three of them. Maybe he thought the other hunter would rat him out so he figured he'd just take all three of them out. Ted roped the other hunter." Hal chuckled. "Chase said that was a sight to see."

She smiled, glad Ted could use his roping skills to take down a bad guy. "I couldn't get any cell phone reception. Not even up on top of the cliff. How did you get word about the shootout?"

"We heard the shooting. Chase hadn't reported in on his radio when he was supposed to. We figured there was trouble. Are you all right?"

"Yeah, you came in the nick of time. Sims and his buddies had shown up and he and Clayton climbed over the fence. They were supposed to pick up Fenton and the other guy, then they saw the Land Rovers and figured you'd caught the men."

"Hell."

"Yeah. I was worried. They were planning to climb the cliffs to get cell phone reception. I was hiding because I wasn't sure how they would react if they found me up there. Anyway, they said they were still going to find the cougar, to prove it existed, but they were going to wait."

"Did you get a picture of them on this side of the fence?"

"No. They might have seen me, and they were armed with rifles."

"Okay, well we have to make this area off-limits to cougars running for now. And we'll keep up surveillance of the area. I'm sorry that Ted and Chase left you to fend for yourself, but I'm glad you weren't in the middle of the shootout either."

"What about the horses?" Stella should have thought of them sooner.

"They were tied up out of the range of all the shooting. They were fine."

Stella sighed.

"I swear we don't usually have this much trouble."

She smiled at him.

"Really."

"I believe you. Maybe I'm just bad luck." That's what she was beginning to think. If the men hadn't believed the white cougar was still on the property, they wouldn't have sent more hunters to try and kill it or bag it or whatever they planned to do with it.

"You're not bad luck. We've had issues before. Every situation is different."

"Maybe we could make a Photoshopped version of a white cougar and share it, saying these hunters had killed it. Maybe they would get some bad publicity for it. And that would be the end of anyone coming to kill it."

"But then we would be saying the men hadn't made it up or imagined what they had done was real. And their lawyer would want to see the body of the cougar for evidence they had shot it."

"Oh, true. That wouldn't work. I just thought if people believed it was gone, no one would bother the ranch and the lands any longer."

When they finally reached the ranch, she saw Ted coming out of the barn where he must have put up the horses. He raced to hug her.

"Ohmigod, Ted, I was so worried about you and Chase." She hugged and kissed him. "Are you both really okay?"

"Yeah, we are. Sorry it took us so long to come and get you. I would have, but Hal said he could get there faster, and I needed to take the horses in."

"Be sure and tell him about Sims," Hal said. "I'm off to talk to Chase and Dan about it." Then Hal took off.

Stella hadn't wanted to talk to Ted about what had happened to her when it was nothing like what had happened to him and Chase with regard to the wanted criminal. But it was better if it came from her first.

Ted took her inside the bunkhouse and they both got some water to drink. Then she explained what had happened to her.

Ted's face turned a little red and she smelled the anger he was feeling about the men being so close to her again, and maybe that they had been a danger to her. "Damn, Stella, I thought you would have been safe where you were." Then he told her what had happened to him and Chase. "Fenton began shooting at us and we had to protect his partner because the guy was shooting at all three of us. His partner wanted his rifle back and the handcuffs off so he could shoot back, but that wasn't happening. If Fenton had killed us, the other guy would have to have taken his chances, but we couldn't risk freeing him and then him shooting us in the back. Then I finally managed to get a shot off and hit Fenton in the shoulder. I swear I heard the bone shatter. Maybe his shooting days are over, if he manages to get himself out of the murder charges he's up on in Denver. Though he'll be charged with his crimes here too."

"Did his hunting partner know he was wanted for murder?"

"No. He was shocked, and he said he knew Fenton wasn't just trying to kill us, but him too. He's eager to testify at the trial against him," Ted said.

"Oh, I forgot to mention, a bear shifter named Blue came to tell me what was going on with you guys. Scared me to pieces when he showed up and then stood up. I was afraid he would climb up the rocks and fight me or something. Anyway, then he shifted and said he was friends with you and the others in Yuma Town. But he heard the shooting you all were doing and left to help, I think, before Sims and his cohorts in crime arrived."

"Hell, it's a good thing Sims and the others didn't see him."

"I agree."

"I need to take a shower."

"Do you want to do a solo shower or—"

"With you if you're agreeable. I need to think of something else. I won't be able to quit thinking about you being alone when Sims and the other men showed up."

"I would have called for help, but my cell phone wouldn't work."

"We need to get some more of those satellite phones. Chase had said his wasn't working, so he needs to replace it."

Ted and Stella took a nice hot shower, soaping each other down, kissing, rinsing off, but not making love in the shower. Some other time would be fine, but they both had just been through an experience and a half, and they needed to just chill.

"Do you want to watch a movie?" Ted asked.

"A romantic comedy. No wild west shootouts this time, or thrillers, or dark dystopian."

"You got it," Ted said.

They got dressed, then ended up in the living room with a bag of popcorn and curled up together, a blanket over the two of them, glasses of water, and the movie that promised to make them laugh.

"Are the horses okay? I asked Hal. He said they were, but I worried about them with all the shooting."

"They're not gun shy and they were way out of range."

"Okay, good." Then she finally relaxed and enjoyed the popcorn, cuddling with Ted, and the movie, glad they had gone for the ride to see the cliffs, which she'd hoped would reassure her that it was safe now to go there. But maybe, with this latest roundup of hunters, they wouldn't have any more hunters entering the property—not if they figured they would be arrested too. Not that Sims and his buddies would stop trying, but it was easier to go after three men, than a bunch of different ones if he should hire others to accomplish the mission.

"You know eventually, if the cat died, the vultures would feast on it and it would be gone. So they're going to have to figure the cougar won't be around much longer," Ted said.

She hadn't planned to say any more about it, just enjoy the movie, but like him, she was still thinking about it. "Right. But if they think they didn't kill it, they could still keep looking for it, just to prove they had truly shot a white cougar."

"I understand what you mean. What would you like to do now?" Ted asked.

"Is it too cold for a barbecue on the back patio?"

"It's never too cold for grilling. I've even done it when it's been snowing."

She laughed.

"Seriously. I had the steaks, the plans, and the snow came in early. I wasn't going to let that stop me."

"I love you."

He chuckled. "I love you too, honey. So what do you want grilled?"

"Chicken legs, if you've got them. I've been feeling like having them for a while."

"Chicken legs it is."

"I'll make us mashed potatoes and gravy and—"

"Brussel sprouts?" he asked.

"Sure, that sounds good. Not to change the subject, but that's scary about the pot growers in the area. I've read where people have been killed who come across the plants in state or federal parks," Stella said.

"Yeah, the first time we found acres of the plants growing in sprout form, we got rid of them in a hurry. Some of us were running as cougars and smelled the plants growing and followed our noses. A couple of growers were sleeping there in a tent and I stayed with Hal to watch them while Tracey ran back to the ranch house by herself to call up the troops. We couldn't do anything to them until we had agents in human form to arrest the men."

"Were the men armed?"

"They were. People like that are dangerous. They make so much money from those crops that they'll kill anyone without any remorse at all."

"Have you ever had to kill anyone who fought back?"

"Yeah. It's our property and our lives at stake. If they won't give up and choose to shoot first, we aren't taking any chances. The thing we've found is that rather than them pushing the issue and attempting to grow the illegal crops on the Halvertons' land, once they have the problem with us, they realize it's a losing battle for them and they cease and desist. We're not just a horse ranch, but a unified cougar community. Not to say that we won't ever have an issue with it at some later date. We might. Which is why we keep an eye on it. They never come anywhere near the horse ranch though. We have too much activity going on there."

"Good."

"What did you want to do for the rest of the afternoon?" Ted asked.

She noticed the clouds were beginning to form again and she suspected they were going to get a repeat of yesterday's afternoon storms.

"It looks like more storms might be coming in this afternoon. So after grilling, we can watch a show? And whatever else that comes to mind." Taking a nap came to mind because they had made love a couple of times during the night as if to make up for the two weeks she would be gone. And of course if they took a nap, they would just have to make love too.

He smiled at her. "You read my mind."

Rather than barbecue the chicken, Ted made lemon and pepper chicken that was absolutely out of this world. Once they cleaned up the grill and put it under wraps, the clouds were darkening, worsening, streaks of lightning shooting down to strike the ground off in the distance.

"We timed that right," she said, grabbing the last of the plates and cups from the patio table before the rain came down in sheets, hitting the patio cover and Ted closed the door against the blowing rain. They laughed and hugged each other after they put the dishes and cups in the dishwasher.

Then the electricity shuddered and went out. It was still daylight, but it was dark because of the pounding storm.

"Bed, then the movie, if our electricity comes on after we're done taking a nap and whatever else we can come up with." Ted chased her into the bedroom.

They made love, napped, and finally woke to find that the electricity was back on. Snuggling on the couch, they watched a movie and she wondered how it would be to stay here with Kolby in residence also. It wouldn't be quite the same. After the movie, Ted and she went over house plans and they decided on one they both loved with an open kitchen/living room arrangement, a master bedroom and bath, and five bedrooms—one for an office, one for a game room, and the other three for guests when Ted's family came to visit and for kids when they had some.

"The dogs will stay with us, won't they, once we move into the house?" she asked.

"You bet, but don't be surprised if Kolby starts asking Hal if he can have a dog too."

Stella laughed. "As long as we have our two. Oh, and a garden wall, just like Tracey has with the fancy garden gates too."

"Naturally." Ted kissed her.

She loved how Ted was a man of action and the first thing he did was call up a contractor—a cougar—who would build the house of their dreams.

CHAPTER 17

"Are you sure you don't want me to come with you and stay the night tonight?" Ted hated for Stella to go home alone that night. He couldn't believe how much he felt he would miss her if she wasn't here with him, and he wouldn't care anything about the commute while being able to be with her.

"Friday, you have to come and stay with me."

"Okay." But Friday was a long time off, he felt. He didn't want to crowd her. Maybe she needed the time to herself to gather her thoughts, pack, and she didn't need him as a distraction. Maybe she needed to unwind from work and wanted to do it alone.

He wanted to have dinner with her, make love to her, go to sleep with her and he wanted to wake up to her in the morning and cuddle with her. He loved her.

"We'll be together shortly. Truly." But when she left him, he knew she wasn't as immune to being with him as she seemed to be, and she tried to hide her tears before she left.

He texted Kolby and said, "Stella has gone home."

"Okay, the other men and I are about finished with chores."

"I'll come out and help you." Ted had to get his mind off Stella, at least for the moment. When he went to bed tonight, she would be all he thought of.

* * *

STELLA HADN'T WANTED TED to have to make that commute day in, day out. Not that she didn't want to come home to him at night, or make love to him, or sleep through the night with him. But she just didn't want him to have to leave at oh-dark-thirty to get up and arrive at the ranch in time to work. It would be different when she lived at the ranch, and he could just fall out of bed, dress, eat and go to work and she would go in later when her day started. His days were much longer too since he had to do some night chores also.

So it was better this way. If he could get off next weekend, they could spend the whole time together. She just hoped it would be okay with the Havertons. They had done so much for them already, she didn't want to impose.

Still, by the time she went to bed that night, all she could think of was Ted and him wrapping his arms around her and kissing her goodnight. Friday wouldn't come soon enough.

* * *

WHEN STELLA RETURNED to work to give notice Monday morning, the lawyers she worked for had to look up the new one she was going to work for.

"From Denver. Why in the world would Larry Pierce open a practice in some hole-in-the-wall location like Yuma Town?" one of the lawyers asked. "Why would you?"

"He's tired of the city life, and his remaining family lives there. As for me, I've met a man I truly care about." She smiled. And they're all cougars, like me, she wanted to add. That's what made living there so special.

"You'll be bored out of your skull," one of the other paralegals said.

"I don't think so." She could just imagine having lunches with Ted and the other ladies, doing a million things with the cougars while there. She spent most of her evenings watching TV series or reading books, wanting to really enjoy life, and now she could. She would still watch TV with Ted, but she'd also go horseback riding and run as a cougar, enjoying the camaraderie of the cougar families. Everyone was already talking about Thanksgiving, and she couldn't be gladder to finally have a real family to have dinner with.

Half the time, she made one of those turkey breasts for dinner and ate it afterwards in soups and sandwiches. But this time? She was eating a whole turkey with a whole family. She couldn't wait for her two weeks to be up so she could return to Yuma Town, that was feeling a lot more like home than this place ever did, no matter how many years she'd lived here.

"Really," one of the other paralegals said to her as the lawyers went off to defend court cases and she and her friend were alone, "why would you leave this job for a little town with a small population that can't have much in the line of real cases? Was the lawyer nearly disbarred and that's why he left the big city?"

None of them would ever understand the cougar's reasoning. "When you fall in love someday, you'll understand."

Tori scoffed. "That's like an every-other-day occurrence for me. I can't imagine uprooting my whole life to go to live in some town in the boondocks." Then she smiled. "Wait, it's all about you living the fantasy of the old west, right?"

"I will be living on a large working horse ranch."

"The guy you're seeing is a cowboy?"

"Foreman of the ranch."

"I've never dated a cowboy. Maybe once you get settled in, you could hook me up with one. Just so I could say I dated one."

Stella smiled. "The other one I know who isn't married is in his twenties, a little young for you."

"Hey, I've been known to be a cougar before."

Stella chuckled. Not like any of them were.

Then a woman came bearing white roses and they had to be from Ted, but Stella didn't want to claim them if they weren't and embarrass herself. "These are for Stella White."

"Oh, thanks so much." Stella put the vase of roses on her desk. They smelled like a delightful perfume.

"Wow," Tori said. "Looks like someone got shot in just the right place."

Stella laughed. "Yeah, though when I was first shot, I didn't think so at all."

* * *

THAT NIGHT after giving her resignation first thing on Monday morning at work—and the paralegals working with Stella had still questioned her sanity, she was surprised to hear a rapping at her apartment door. She hung up her suit jacket on the coat rack and when she looked through the peephole, there was her cowboy, all smiling, Stetson on his head, and white roses in his hand.

Stella beamed. She just couldn't believe it. She opened the door and pulled Ted into her apartment, kissing him at the same time, locked her door, then pulled his Stetson off and set it on her coat rack. "I never expected seeing you here."

"I couldn't stop thinking about you and I wanted to see how they had treated you after you gave them your resignation."

"Ha! You were worried I wouldn't have the nerve to resign." She began unsnapping the snaps on his western shirt, forget trying to figure out something for dinner to eat alone.

"No. I knew you couldn't wait to return to Yuma Town, and you wouldn't have put Larry in a bind, when he knows you're working for him in two weeks. And you would miss me too much unless you had changed your mind about you and me."

"No way." She was kissing Ted again, pulling his shirt off his shoulders, remembering she needed to unsnap the long sleeves of his shirt first. Then she yanked them free and pulled his shirt off the rest of the way and kissed his shoulders, his pecs, his scruffy chin, then met his mouth again with hers, kissing smartly, then deepening the kiss.

* * *

TED HAD ACHED to be with her even when he was working hard on the job. She was like a thirst he couldn't quench. Now they were together again, and the need had intensified all the more. In life and love, he would give her everything—commitment, protection, loving, sharing, caring. He was so happy to be with her, relieved even. He hoped once she moved in with him, he wouldn't feel this desperate to see her, knowing they would be together every night and when she wasn't working.

Her scent of woman and she-cat and intrigue and sex took his breath away, held him in hungry anticipation. He pressed his hands over her breasts and felt her nipples, tight peaks pressing against her clothes and his hands.

He pulled her close, their bodies flush, her breathing and his ragged with lust. They kissed and her tongue darted out to lick his mouth, and he invited her in, wanting the connection, the anticipation of being with her like this again feeling better than right. She deepened the kiss and hugged him tight.

"I've wanted to do this since I left you. I'm glad you came here and didn't wait."

"You know it," he said, sweeping his hands through her hair. "I didn't want to dream about being with you. I wanted to live it."

"Oh, I so agree."

A swirling, heady maelstrom of need rushed through his

bloodstream, and a low groan rumbled forth from deep within his throat as he slid his hand up her skirt covering her thigh and she ran her hands over the front of his jeans, cupping his sex.

He had given her his heart, his body, his strength, his soul. He was hers forever. She kissed him with the kind of passion like he knew she would, just like he gave her back.

She took a deep breath and smiled up at him. "I figured I'd bring some of my stuff to the ranch on the weekend to join you. I didn't think you'd be coming here during the week to see me. Not that I'm disappointed to say the least. I just didn't want you to have to make that commute so early in the morning."

"I can't stay away from you. Besides, this is a dangerous place to live," he explained, running his hand over her shoulders. He said it just in case she had any real objection to him being here. "I would be remiss not to be here to make sure you remain safe—at least at night." In truth, he couldn't stay away from her for anything.

CHAPTER 18

"So you're staying the night?" Stella asked, breathlessly, their kisses renewing. She had thought maybe Ted was going to come just for dinner, make love, then he would return home again as early as he had to get up to work at the ranch.

"Yeah. Boss Man and Boss Lady expected it of me. They wouldn't have it any other way. The two new ranch hands are really working out and well, what can I say? I can't get enough of being with you." He ran his hands over her blouse covered breasts. "Of this."

"Your overnight bag is in the truck?" She still couldn't believe he was planning to stay the night without telling her. Luckily, the place was clean. Though she should have started to pack or something.

Getting in late Sunday night and working all day Monday had kind of quashed the notion of packing. She'd actually planned to get some done every night. Tonight, even.

"Yeah, as long as you're fine with it."

She smiled at him. "Oh, absolutely. You can help me pack." Though that's not what she really wanted to do with him right this moment. She resumed kissing and he began unbuttoning her blouse.

She hadn't even had time to change out of her business suit for work. At least she'd ditched her pumps and her suit jacket once she'd arrived home.

He removed her blouse and kissed her shoulders. "Hmm, I missed you last night."

She smiled and began working on his belt. "I missed you too." Though she had to admit she'd been worn out by all the activities this past weekend and all their lovemaking and she suspected her wounds and rattlesnake bite had had something to do with that too.

But once she was with him again, it was like he rejuvenated every cell in her body and she was raring to go. "I think you're just perfect for me."

"I know you are for me."

Not that they wouldn't have disagreements with each other. She wondered how building a house would go. But maybe he wouldn't care as long as she was happy with it. And truly, anything would be nicer than her ultra-tiny apartment. Which, for a single woman or man was fine, but she was ready for more —a family, and even more of an extended family. For having parties, dinner engagements at the house, yeah, that would be totally fine.

Then he was pulling off her skirt and she was wearing only her panties and bra—plain white, no frills. She hadn't expected her macho cougar to show up at her house tonight or she might have gone for sexier and more enticing. He didn't seem to notice, his hands on her breasts, his mouth on hers again.

Then she was moving her hands down to his belt again, tackling it, and unfastening it. She unfastened his jeans, but he hurried to lean down and jerk his cowboy boots and socks off. Then she was pulling down his jeans and he was kissing her mouth again, his hands on her breasts, massaging, making her feel sexy and needed.

She ran her hand over his boxer briefs as he kicked aside his jeans.

Then he picked her up and she wrapped her legs around his hips, and he carried her into the—"Bedroom to the right," she said, as he almost took her into the spare bedroom turned into an office.

He set her on her feet on the floor in the bedroom and peeled her bra straps off her shoulders, kissing each shoulder before he reached around to unfasten the bra in back, a normal reaction, only the fastener was in the front. She moved his hand around the front, and he smiled and unsnapped it. Then he pulled her bra off, cupped her breasts, and kissed her mouth.

She cupped his buttocks and pulled him flush against her, kissing his mouth, tonguing him, loving him.

He was soon stripping off her panties, pulling them off all the way as she rested her hands on his shoulders to balance herself. Then she was pulling off his boxer briefs and they were on the bed, kissing, moving against each other, his hands cupping her face while she moved a leg over the back of his thigh and rubbed at him.

He groaned and slipped his hand between them and began to stroke her nub. Just breathing in his cougar scent and him, their pheromones dancing around each other, enticing each other, his touching her and his warm breath against her skin catapulted her into a climax.

She wrapped both her legs around him and he plunged into her, going deep, thrusting, just as into her as she was into him.

"I love you," she said, not afraid to tell him that every time she was with him or missing him.

"I love you too," he said, his voice rough with need as he paused to kiss her mouth, and then he was thrusting again.

She knew he would make love to her again tonight. She could count on it. He had stamina, just like she knew a cowboy would.

He continued to thrust, and finally came, groaning out her name in a loving way. "Oh, man, Stella, you are the only one for me, ever."

"I feel the same way about you."

They kissed again and then he finally pulled out, and he wrapped his arms around her.

She sighed. "This couldn't have been a better pick-me-up."

He chuckled. "I agree."

They were spent, feeling satiated, lying tangled together, loving each other.

She loved him without reservation, knowing he was the only one for her, that she had finally found a home with a man who loved her unconditionally. A white cougar, an oddity, but to him, she was perfect, and he was the same for her.

"Love you, you big old cat. I hope you realize what we'll be doing again later tonight." She was overjoyed that he'd come to be with her and like usual, had made her life better than it would have been if he hadn't been here for her tonight.

"You can count on it." He smiled at her and kissed her again.

"Hmm, you are not going to be conducive to sleep."

He chuckled. "I know I'll sleep better being with you."

"Not me, being with you. I'll want to wake you up in the middle of the night." She kissed his beautiful bare chest. "I was going to just grab something to eat out of the fridge when I got off work, but do you want to go out and celebrate?"

"I sure do. Where's the best steakhouse around?"

"My favorite—Philly's Steakhouse. I'll drive." She wanted to enjoy the places she always went to by herself with him now.

"This looks good," he said, when they arrived at the restaurant and went inside. "Smells good too."

"They have the best steaks." They were ushered to a table. "I still can't believe you're here."

"I couldn't stay away." He smiled. "All I thought of all day was being with you all night."

"I'm glad you came tonight. If I'd had any doubts you were the right one for me, that dispelled them," she said.

"No way would I have let you think that. I did briefly think that you might need the time to have on your own, but that was such a fleeting thought that before you know it, I was telling Hal I was on my way to Grand Junction. He said he was glad because the place is dangerous."

She smiled. "Really, I've never had any trouble."

After they had a steak dinner, they returned to her apartment to watch a western.

That night, they went to bed and made love, a beautiful ending to a surprise visit, but poor Ted had to leave really early for work the next morning because of the hour drive too. Even though he said Hal and Kolby said they would cover things as they were training the new ranch hands, Ted wanted to get there at his usual time for starting work.

But Stella didn't have to get up that early. They'd made love after the movie before bed and she was still tired. Still, she got up and fixed them waffles and sausages while wearing a nighty and robe and slippers and he was dressed to do cowboy duties at the ranch.

"I'll see you tonight, and every night until you've moved to the ranch," he promised.

"I would love nothing more, but if it gets to be too much, you don't have to."

"It's only for two weeks. It won't be any time at all, and it will go by all the faster if I come at night to see you. I can bring you some boxes too and help you to pack up whatever you need me to haul over in the meantime."

"Thanks, though I was going to pick some up at one of the stores where they dump their clean boxes for the trash—"

"No! Don't do that." Ted sounded so serious, she wondered why that wasn't a good idea.

"You don't mean to tell me you tried to get discarded boxes and the store staff thought you were stealing merchandise or something, do you?"

"No, Bridget and Travis met over such a situation though."

"They're happily mated." At least that's what Stella had heard.

"Travis was grabbing some boxes to use to move his household goods, and overhead the men running the store making criminal plans. They knocked him out and tied him up and thankfully for Travis, Bridget found him and freed him, though she wasn't sure he wasn't just a bad guy too to begin with. Being that you live in a dangerous city, I'd rather you didn't go diving for clean boxes behind shops also."

Stella closed her gaping mouth. "Okay, you bring me some boxes."

He smiled. "That's exactly what I'll do." He finished his coffee and then pulled Stella into a hug. "I'll see you tonight."

"I look forward to it."

"And I'll spend the weekend here helping you to get packed."

Which was a good thing because by the time the weekend had arrived, they hadn't packed one box, though Ted was good at his word and had been bringing packing boxes every night, some of which smelled of sweet vanilla cooking dough, heavenly, from Fitzgerald's bakery. They were too busy—making love, getting dinner, watching a movie, and sometimes it was even something other than a western—like catching up on the *Mandalorian* series, and making love and sleeping—to do anything else all week long.

Saturday, they went through her things and she was hanging onto stuff she could use in the new house—small kitchen appliances, though Ted told her they could ask for new ones at the bridal shower. Since they were going to be living at the bunkhouse for several months while the house was built, she capitulated and was giving away all the items to the local Women's Crisis Center.

"I rented the furnished apartment, so we don't have to do anything with the furniture." She packed away all her knick-knacks and anything else she wouldn't need to use for the next week—her summer clothes mainly.

On Monday following the weekend, Ted moved all the packed boxes in his pickup to the ranch to work that day, so she didn't have packing boxes all over the apartment and she was glad for that. At lunchtime, she was dropping the boxes of donated items off at the Women's Crisis Center.

Ted was also meeting with the builder to start work on the house and she couldn't wait to see the building going on once it began, all the way through the finishing touches. She'd never seen anything like that, and it would be just one more fun experience she'd have with Ted.

"I want everything similar to what the bunkhouse has in the line of an open living room and the island counter, the cabinets and countertops, tile backsplash and the bedroom too. I just love it. And horse pictures. The works."

"We'll have it all," Ted promised her.

Then he was off on the last lap of their journey, she felt, and at the beginning of a new one.

That Monday morning, she was back to work, getting through the days, and had a party on Friday to say farewell. Ted was invited, and all the ladies wanted to see the cowboy who had swept Stella off her feet. And Ted, being the good-natured guy that he was, would be there early, Hal and Tracey telling him if he didn't take off from work—owing to his own work ethic—they would drive him themselves. Though they had considered doing so anyway, to help move the last of Stella's things to the ranch.

Stella had wrestled with herself over when she would actually move to the ranch. Should they stay another couple of nights at the apartment and have the weekend to themselves because if

Ted and she were at the ranch, he would be doing some work? Or just get it over with and move the rest of her household goods, leaving her more human life behind and getting into the swing of things with her cougar friends?

But she still hadn't decided and figured Ted would help her to decide.

On Friday, they had a fun send off at the office party. It was a short day for her, and everyone cheered her for her help and the ladies asked Ted if there were any more eligible bachelor cowboys staying at the ranch. She swore she had never seen the tips of Ted's ears turn so red. He seemed to be embarrassed by all the attention he was getting. But after they said their goodbyes and Ted shook the lawyers' hands and the women gave him and Stella hugs, they finally headed to the apartment.

"Okay, so the question is should we stay at the apartment overnight and leave tomorrow or Sunday even, or should we just pack it all up and move tonight?" Stella asked.

"I'd really like to pack it up, horseback ride with you tomorrow, see the sun set out at the ranch, have a barbecue with just you and me at the bunkhouse."

She smiled. That sounded really nice. She didn't know why she was even considering staying another minute at the apartment. "Okay, that sounds so good."

"And don't worry about me working over the weekend. I have no weekend duty—Hal and Tracey's orders."

She sighed. "Good. I was afraid of that. I guess since it's earlier than I normally leave work or that you get here, we can just pack up the vehicles and go to the ranch and have dinner there."

"That's just what I was thinking."

When they arrived at the apartment, she was excited about turning in her key. She still had another two weeks that she could stay at the apartment, but she was glad to be leaving. She unlocked the door, and they went inside. Usually, they would stop to kiss, but she was on a mission. He caught up with her and kissed her anyway. He smiled down at her. "I'm so lucky to have you."

"Oh, me too, to have you." Then she kissed him back and hugged him tight.

"Once we're all settled in, I want to take you to the Buchanan's Carver Falls too. They're beautiful falls, but a little far to travel even on cougar foot from the ranch. So I was thinking, we could rent a cabin on a Friday night and stay the weekend—and explore as cougars at night around the area. I would love to do the same with you during summer, sometime, and we can go swimming and boating on the lake. But for now?"

"We can do it and have a place of our 'own' and give Kolby and the other ranch hands the bunkhouse for their own for a weekend. I'd love it."

Afterwards, they were in a hurry to carry out the rest of the boxes of stuff to their vehicles. She was carrying another box to her Jeep while Ted was getting one from her bedroom when the three hunters who had shot her moved out of the shadows and surrounded her.

"At the trial, you need to tell the jury," Sims said, "you never seen who shot you. Just remember it's your word against ours." He had her backed up against her Jeep, the box of clothes in her arms keeping him at bay, but she didn't know if he was armed or not.

"Sure," she said, because it wasn't a good idea to antagonize a man who could be wearing a concealed weapon. But the thing is, she hadn't seen who was shooting because she was in the barn!

Braxton moved in close to her, as if she didn't get the message loud and clear. "Yeah, listen to Sims. If you don't want to see us again, and I'll tell you right now, none of the charges are going to hold up, you'll tell them that we didn't do anything."

They were crazy! If they wanted to intimidate anyone, they would have to do it with the others who were there—Ted, Larry,

Kolby, and Tracey—who had actually witnessed the hunters shooting at the barn!

She wanted to tell them she was moving to a heavily fortified ranch and they were welcome to come harass her there, but she knew to keep her mouth shut. She hoped Ted was coming out soon so they knew she wasn't here all by herself.

Clayton had to add his two cents. "We're hunters and we love the sport of killing. If you get my meaning."

Could they make their threat any clearer?

The other two men chuckled. Then Sims said, "You know, we don't want to lose our hunting licenses, that's what Clayton's referring to."

But she knew that wasn't what they were saying at all. Not that they would actually kill her, but that they were definitely threatening her with that. She should have just ignored them, but she was getting riled up that they wouldn't let her move her box into her Jeep, that they were in her space, and they were threatening her.

"Why don't you repeat what you said to me here at the trial. See how the jury takes your 'comments' then."

CHAPTER 19

*A*s soon as Ted heard one of the hunters who had shot Stella threatening her, he was outside in a flash, no packing box in hand, and unfortunately, he wasn't armed with a rifle like before, but he had his phone out and was video recording all of it surreptitiously. "I've called the police. Stay here and they'll arrest you for intimidating a witness." He'd already called the police and he'd called his own friends, just in case they needed their help. Now he wished he'd gone along with Hal and Tracey's offer of help earlier to move Stella's household goods, since they were both law enforcement officers.

"My brother's a cop and his friends are my friends," Sims said.

The problem was that locally, they might be, and Ted and Stella didn't have a prayer of getting justice here if these men were friends with the police force. But in Yuma Town, where they'd shot Stella, that was a different story. They wouldn't win there.

"Fine, then they'll escort you out of here." Ted hadn't been telling a tall tale either. Not only had he called the local police, who he didn't know if he could trust, but he had called Sheriff Dan that he and Stella were in trouble and gave the address. They wouldn't be able to get here for an hour, but at least they would have an escort to Yuma Town.

"Why don't you men just get out of our face and let us get on with business," Ted said, his voice turning growly.

"Don't tell us you're running like scared little rabbits," Sims said, motioning to the boxes, as if he hadn't realized at first what that was all about.

Rabbits? More like big cougars who would take these guys out in a heartbeat if they could, Ted thought.

"You're the guy who went into the barn to kill the white cougar," Sims finally said. "We know it was in the barn."

"Yeah, well, we have nothing to say about the court case. That will be for a judge and jury to handle," Ted said.

A couple of cop cars finally pulled up and Ted took Stella's box of clothes and put it in her vehicle.

"So what's the problem here, Sims?" the one officer asked.

Ted waited for him to tell the cop the truth. He wasn't sure if the men were related. They didn't look like it. His brother might not have been able to make the call.

"Nothing," Sims said. "We just noticed the lady was carrying her stuff out to the car and we offered to help. Then this guy gets all hot and bothered, tells us we have no business hassling his girlfriend and—"

"Why don't you tell the officer the truth, Sims? That you shot her in the barn on the ranch where I'm a foreman and she was in the clinic for the wounds she suffered. That you're up on charges for assault with a deadly weapon, attempted murder, and could have killed or injured four-year-old quadruplets and their mother while you were shooting everything in sight? That you were just now intimidating Ms. White from testifying against you?"

"That's a lie," Sims said.

"Are you leaving?" the officer asked Stella.

"Yeah, I'm just packing up my things now," Stella said.

"Why don't you finish your business and get on your way," the officer said, acting like Stella was the troublemaker, not the men threatening her.

"I will, if these men will stop threatening me."

"Sims, you and your buddies leave, now." The officer waited for the men to reluctantly get in the truck, slam the doors, and tear off. "You need to get out of here and stay away."

Stella said, "I intend to. Thanks for coming to our aid." Then she headed back inside the apartment to finish packing up, shaking from the experience.

Ted glowered at the officer.

"You too."

Then Ted inclined his head and walked back inside and locked the door and hugged Stella. He wanted to always be her protector.

"What if the hunters follow us and try to run us off the road or something?" Stella asked, sounding afraid.

He wasn't surprised. No telling what the men would do and with her being alone, he wouldn't trust that they were through with causing trouble for her tonight. "The troops are coming. Like I said, we have your back. Not just me, but a whole lot of cougars in town. Everyone really. But we have enough law enforcement in town to protect our own. They'll be our escort home."

She wrapped her arms around his neck and kissed him soundly. "Oh, God, thank you. I was so worried they'd try to kill us both and no one would ever know the truth."

"Nope. And we never show our hand when we don't have to. I recorded everything that was being said." He showed her his phone, and the recording on it.

She watched the video and then smiled at him. "I would never have thought of doing that. Thanks for coming to my rescue."

"I'm just glad they hadn't come earlier when I wasn't here."

"You are the greatest."

He smiled. "I didn't want them to get away with intimidating a witness and for the local police department to ignore it. At least Sims and his buddies will have some more charges filed against them this weekend. It just pisses me off that some lawyer bailed them out and that the judge set the bail to allow it."

She hugged him tight, then let out her breath. "Do we continue to pack up the vehicles or—"

"Our escort will help us so we don't have any other issues tonight. Just in case Sims and his friends send some other thugs to harass us."

"Okay, great." Then they went into the bedroom and packed up all the remaining items and she checked her bathroom one last time. They did another check through the kitchen and all the cabinets and fridge, then checked her office. They only had another five boxes to haul out to the vehicles and he really had just wanted to get on their way, but he didn't trust that they would be safe.

It took an hour for the troops to arrive, and he was hoping it was quiet in Yuma Town, but deputy sheriffs Chase, Hal, Ricky, Stryker, and Nina were there. Sheriff Dan had come to oversee things also. Tracey had stayed home with the kids. But Travis, Jack, and Leyton with the Cougar Special Forces were there too. With the new video evidence that showed Sims and his buddies threatening Stella, the hunters would land back in jail, no bailing them out this time. Maybe, they would learn their lesson that they couldn't bully their way out of criminal charges. So even though the men had scared her, Ted's quick thinking had taken care of the men.

It took a couple of minutes for them to carry the rest of the boxes out to Stella's Jeep, and then Nina rode with her in her Jeep to protect her. Dan took Stella's key to the apartment manager to drop it off.

And then the caravan of police cars and Ted and Stella's vehicles were on their way.

* * *

STELLA STILL COULDN'T BELIEVE how wonderful everyone was in coming to their aid. At one point, she saw Sim and his friends in their black truck parked close to her apartment complex, but they probably didn't believe all the police traffic going into the complex was for her benefit. She smiled. They wouldn't dare try to intimidate her again. Besides the fact they would be going to jail and their bond revoked soon.

"So what do you think about our town and the people who live there?" Nina asked.

Stella smiled at her. "You all are the best. Thanks for coming to my rescue."

"I'm just glad Ted was there for you before the men showed up. You can always call on us, no matter where you are, and we'll be there for you. Guaranteed."

That was a great feeling, and she knew she'd made the right decision in agreeing to mate Ted and join the cougar families of Yuma Town.

When they arrived at the ranch, everyone wished them well, Tracey and the kids hugged them, and that was the beginning of a new life not only for Stella, but for Ted too.

EPILOGUE

*S*tella had always felt the issue with her being a white cougar set her at a disadvantage. Both because she would be a remarkable cougar to kill and for some hunter to brag about, but also because she was afraid no cougar would ever want her for a mate. Sure, that was because of her father always putting her down, but it made her believe all men would. And since she'd mostly dated humans, she really hadn't known how a cougar would feel about it. But with Ted, he'd been nothing but accepting and she couldn't have been more grateful to have found him and fallen head over heels for him. Like her, he'd had issues with a hateful father, and she loved how sweet he was with the Haverton kids, and others he worked with when they came out to the ranch to get riding lessons or just play. He would make a great father, she felt. And she was proud to have him for her mate.

Even today with everyone getting ready to have a big barbecue between Halloween and Thanksgiving, he was out there chasing the kids around, pretending to lasso them. When he wasn't doing that, he was teaching the other ones how to lasso a post, just to get the hang of it. She loved watching him having fun with the kids.

She loved riding with him too, and Hal and Tracey were giving her Celestina, the beautiful chestnut appaloosa she'd fallen in love with since the first day Ted had taken her for a ride on her.

The trial for Jeffrey Sims and his hunting buddies was scheduled for three months from now and Ted, Larry, Tracey, Kolby, and Bill, who would be flying in to take part, would be eyewitnesses for the prosecution. Three months after that, their home would be finished, and she and Ted couldn't wait to furnish it and move in.

The wedding was scheduled for two weeks after Christmas, and everyone wanted to come! She had learned that being a white cougar here, meant she was no longer a pariah. And she was glad for that. Thankfully, the new ranch hands and Kolby loved her cooking when she made meals for all the cowboys, and she loved Ted and Kolby's cooking too. They told her often enough, they would miss her when she moved with Ted to their home overlooking the river, but she knew Kolby was looking forward to taking over the master bedroom. She noted that the two new ranch hands hadn't said the same about Ted, though they all liked him, because he was also their boss and she figured they would feel freer to do what they wanted without him keeping an eye on them at the bunkhouse. But Ted had already told Kolby he had the job of keeping them in line if he needed to —since he was now the old hand. And Kolby was glad for the leadership role and helping Ted train the new guys.

She and Ted went out daily to check on the house too.

She loved working for Larry Pierce. He was like a father to her, treating her like family, not just an employee, which she hadn't expected. She would have made the worst mistake in her life if she hadn't come here and joined him. He was always full of praise for her.

Ted joined her after he let Kolby take over for him and pulled her into his arms and kissed her. "You're okay with going home to see my family for Thanksgiving, aren't you?"

"Yeah, you know it. I can't wait to see your sister and the rest of the family. I hope your sister is fine with me coming there."

"Are you kidding?" Ted wrapped his arms around her waist, her back to him and rested his hands on her belly. "Sooner or later, we'll be telling her we're having children of our own and she will want to spoil them rotten too. My sister will adore you. I have to say she was thrilled when my nephew, Scott, mated a fellow army officer, Nicole, and now she has a newfound friend to visit with when they come from Fort Hood for family gatherings. They will bring you into the fold and you'll have a great time."

Stella smiled, placing her hands on his. "That will be so nice. I haven't had a female cougar friend in forever, and I'm on the outs with my biological mother for siding with my father against me for being an oddity. And of course I don't have anything to do with my adoptive parents either. It's so nice to feel like part of a family again."

He leaned over her shoulder and kissed her cheek. "You will have a lot of family, including all of the townsfolk of Yuma Town. I was afraid when I first met you, before you even shifted, that you might be a lone cougar. I've met a couple in my lifetime, and they felt safer living on their own, surrounded by humans, and running as cougars when they had time to—but alone. They believed it was sounder to do that, like cougars do, except for mothers with their offspring."

"Except one time there was a news report where a daddy cougar was staying in the den with the mother and her little ones. It had given me a lift to read the heartwarming article. There are exceptions to every rule. And maybe more males do that, but it's just not recorded."

"True. All I know is I'll be there for you when it happens."

She loved Ted for being who he was: genuine, kind, caring, and totally fun to be with.

* * *

TED WAS eager to take Stella home with him, and his sister, Josephine, and niece, Janice, and her boys, Roy and Shawn, were excited to meet her. He knew they had all been exchanging texts and Instagram posts, the boys showing the drawings they had made, his sister showing Stella pictures of the stores she wanted to take her to, her mother making sure she knew just what Stella loved to eat and do before she came for Thanksgiving. And his sister had already bought tickets to see "Texas" at the Palo Duro outdoor theater in Canyon, Texas.

They were going for two weeks, and he had never spent that much time away from the Haverton's ranch, but he needed to do this for his family and for his new mate, and the Havertons were thrilled for him.

Kolby was most of all because he said he would be the foreman while Ted was gone, which had amused Ted.

Ted hugged Stella tighter.

"Hey, we'll still be here for Christmas and last year Kolby and I won the best Christmas tree contest—western themed. So we'll have to be working on that after Thanksgiving when we return home. Though we've got the wedding coming up after that."

"You probably wouldn't win the contest for another western-themed tree though. Maybe we'll have to come up with something different with the other guys. Or, we can just do it since we love western themed anyway."

"We can come up with ideas and put it to a vote," Ted said, glad she was game.

He loved taking Stella on daily rides to see their home built on the river. It would be built by spring, if the holidays and weather didn't cause too much trouble. As much as he loved the newly renovated bunkhouse, it was time to have a home of his own with his mate, and someday, his children. He would still be the foreman for the ranch, though Kolby was eager to move into the master bedroom at the bunkhouse, elevating his living quarter's status, with the additional role of watching out for the new ranch hands.

"Hey, while everyone's busy playing, do you want to sneak away to the bunkhouse?" Ted asked.

"For some more loving? You bet, Cowboy. Whisk me away."

And he did just that, grabbed her up and hauled her off to the bunkhouse to make love to his beautiful and extraordinary mate. He loved her with all his heart.

ACKNOWLEDGMENTS

Thanks so much to Donna Fournier and Darla Taylor for reading over the book and suggesting changes. Darla and I live in Texas, so thinking fall can be hard to do. That's why we need a Minnesota girl to help us see the cold and fall and winter. And that makes it all the more fun. Thanks, Donna, for keeping me straight on more northern climates when I'm writing about locations other than the south! And brainstorming when I need it!!!

You all help to make the books so much better!

AUTHOR BIO

USA Today bestselling author Terry Spear has written over eighty paranormal and medieval Highland romances. In 2008, Heart of the Wolf was named a Publishers Weekly Best Book of the Year. She has received a PNR Top Pick, a Best Book of the Month nomination by Long and Short Reviews, numerous Night Owl Romance Top Picks, and 2 Paranormal Excellence Awards for Romantic Literature (Finalist & Honorable Mention). In 2016, Billionaire in Wolf's Clothing was an RT Book Reviews Top Pick. A retired officer of the U.S. Army Reserves, Terry also creates award-winning teddy bears that have found homes all over the world, helps out with her granddaughter, and soon a grandson, and she is raising two Havanese puppies. She lives in Spring, Texas.

Wild Highland Lass (novella), Vexing the Highlander (novella), My Highlander

Other historical romances: Lady Caroline & the Egotistical Earl, A Ghost of a Chance at Love

* * *

Heart of the Wolf Series: Heart of the Wolf, Destiny of the Wolf, To Tempt the Wolf, Legend of the White Wolf, Seduced by the Wolf, Wolf Fever, Heart of the Highland Wolf, Dreaming of the Wolf, A SEAL in Wolf's Clothing, A Howl for a Highlander, A Highland Werewolf Wedding, A SEAL Wolf Christmas, Silence of the Wolf, Hero of a Highland Wolf, A Highland Wolf Christmas, A SEAL Wolf Hunting; A Silver Wolf Christmas, A SEAL Wolf in Too Deep, Alpha Wolf Need Not Apply, Billionaire in Wolf's Clothing, Between a Rock and a Hard Place, SEAL Wolf Undercover, Dreaming of a White Wolf Christmas, Flight of the White Wolf, All's Fair in Love and Wolf, A Billionaire Wolf for Christmas, SEAL Wolf Surrender (2019), Silver Town Wolf: Home for the Holidays (2019), Wolff Brothers: You Had Me at Wolf, Night of the Billionaire Wolf, Joy to the Wolves (Red Wolf), The Wolf Wore Plaid, Jingle Bell Wolf, Best of Both Wolves

SEAL Wolves: To Tempt the Wolf, A SEAL in Wolf's Clothing, A SEAL Wolf Christmas, A SEAL Wolf Hunting, A SEAL Wolf in Too Deep, SEAL Wolf Undercover, SEAL Wolf Surrender (2019)

Silver Bros Wolves: Destiny of the Wolf, Wolf Fever, Dreaming of the Wolf, Silence of the Wolf, A Silver Wolf Christmas, Alpha Wolf Need Not Apply, Between a Rock and a Hard Place, All's Fair in Love and Wolf, Silver Town Wolf: Home for the Holidays (2019)

Wolff Brothers of Silver Town

Billionaire Wolves: Billionaire in Wolf's Clothing, A Billionaire Wolf for Christmas, Night of the Billionaire Wolf

Highland Wolves: Heart of the Highland Wolf, A Howl for a Highlander, A Highland Werewolf Wedding, Hero of a Highland Wolf, A Highland Wolf Christmas, Wolf Wore Plaid

Red Wolf Series: Seduced by the Wolf, Joy to the Wolves

* * *

Heart of the Jaguar Series: Savage Hunger, Jaguar Fever, Jaguar Hunt, Jaguar Pride, A Very Jaguar Christmas, You Had Me at Jaguar (2019)

Novella: The Witch and the Jaguar (2018)

* * *

Romantic Suspense: Deadly Fortunes, In the Dead of the Night, Relative Danger, Bound by Danger

* * *

Vampire romances: Killing the Bloodlust, Deadly Liaisons, Huntress for Hire, Forbidden Love, Vampire Redemption, Primal Desire

Vampire Novellas: Vampiric Calling, The Siren's Lure, Seducing the Huntress

* * *

Other Romance: Exchanging Grooms, Marriage, Las Vegas Style

* * *

Science Fiction Romance: Galaxy Warrior
Teen/Young Adult/Fantasy Books
The World of Fae:

The Dark Fae, Book 1

The Deadly Fae, Book 2

The Winged Fae, Book 3

The Ancient Fae, Book 4

Dragon Fae, Book 5

Hawk Fae, Book 6

Phantom Fae, Book 7

Golden Fae, Book 8

Falcon Fae, Book 9

Woodland Fae, Book 10

Angel Fae, Book 11 (TBD)

The World of Elf:

The Shadow Elf

Darkland Elf

Blood Moon Series:

Kiss of the Vampire

The Vampire...In My Dreams

Demon Guardian Series:

The Trouble with Demons

Demon Trouble, Too

Demon Hunter

Non-Series for Now:

Ghostly Liaisons

The Beast Within

Courtly Masquerade

Deidre's Secret

The Magic of Inherian:

The Scepter of Salvation

The Mage of Monrovia

Emerald Isle of Mists (TBA)